LIE TO ME

THE CLARKE BROTHERS: BOOK ONE

LILIAN MONROE

~

1

___

MADELINE

"Madeline! My office, now!"

I glance up from my desk and sigh. Barry isn't in a good mood. We're mobilizing to the new construction site next month, and there are a million things to do. I click 'save' on my computer and stand up. My environmental report will have to wait. I turn toward Barry's office and try to keep my face neutral.

Our project director, Barry Atkins, is a middle-aged, gruff-looking man with a big potbelly. He's hunched over at his desk, squinting at his computer when I walk into his office. His eyebrows are knitted together and he's stroking his thick mustache with one hand as he scrolls down the screen with the other.

"Read this," he barks without looking up. I take a few steps to walk around his desk and look at his screen with him. It's an email forwarded on from our community liaison manager at the project site.

I

Barry glances at me and I take a deep breath. He shakes his head.

"The pushback we've been getting from the community is getting worse. They don't want this hotel to be built. I need you to go to Lang Creek and be the company representative for this town hall meeting."

I make a choking, gurgling sound before taking another deep breath.

"Barry, with all due respect, I have three applications to make to state and federal environmental agencies that need to be in by the end of next week. I don't have time to go down there, not now. If I don't get these submitted, we won't be able to start on time. Wouldn't it be better for one of the project engineers to go?"

"Who, Patrick? Glen? They'll make things worse! They'd go in there like they were ordering some workers around on site. No, we need someone with finesse." He looks at me and softens his voice. "We need you. You're the environmental engineer on this project and you're in the best position to put the community's mind at ease. We need to win their hearts and minds. Put a presentation together, and make sure you mention all our sustainability initiatives. Talk about that other project you worked on – the rehabilitation of the old mine site you worked on."

He waves his hand and I take a deep breath to try to calm myself down. I know how important this is, but as the only environmental engineer on this project, my plate is already too full.

"Barry, I need help. We're building this hotel on a Class I Nature reserve, and I have seventeen applications that need to be approved. The three going in next week are going to determine whether we can start on time. I can't –"

Barry swings his eyes up toward me and furrows his brow. I know that look. It's a look that doesn't invite discussion. I gulp and then nod, taking a deep breath to steady my voice.

"I'll get it done," I say.

Barry nods. "Good. I knew I could count on you."

He turns back to his computer and I head back toward my desk. I flop down on my chair and look at my computer screen, dejected. I have a half-finished Noise and Vibration Report, plus a to-do list that's overwhelming to look at. I look around at everyone tapping away on their keyboards and I wonder if they're as overwhelmed as me. Now he wants me to put together a presentation *and* head into the heart of the Adirondack Mountains? I somehow have to win over the Lang Creek County population by Friday? What is our community liaison manager even doing down there!

I've worked with Barry for almost five years now, and I know that he's right. We need to handle the community correctly to save ourselves trouble down the line. But still, sometimes I feel like he relies on me too much. I pull out my Tupperware box from my bag and open it up. Looks like it'll be another lunch eaten alone at my desk as I rush to finish yet another task.

I haven't even stuck my fork into the salad leaves when my phone rings. I check the screen and sigh. It's Cecilia, our community liaison manager.

"Hi Cecilia," I say as I put my fork down and stare blankly at my screen.

"Maddy! Barry told me you'd be leading this town meeting."

"Not sure about leading it, but I'll be there."

"Have you prepared the presentation yet?"

"Cecilia, I just got told I'm going to Lang Creek ten minutes ago. I haven't even opened up PowerPoint yet." I can hear the tension in my voice and I try to take a quiet breath.

"Right, right. I've been having some issues getting people on board," she starts. "They're worried about the hotel construction site to begin with. Then they think it'll bring in too many tourists and the area will be destroyed."

I can tell. "I'll let you know when my presentation is done," I answer curtly. I hang up the phone and rub my hands over my temples. My lunch looks unappetizing, but I stab it with my fork anyway. I munch on a lettuce leaf before looking at my screen. I open up a blank presentation and take a deep breath. I might as well get started working on this.

2

AIDEN

I TAKE a step back and run my eyes over the big pile of neatly stacked firewood. The sweat is beading on my forehead and I can feel it dripping down the center of my back. I unzip the front of my jacket and let the cool air come close to my body. I take a deep breath and nod to myself. This should keep me going for a month at least.

As I'm turning toward the cabin, I hear the crunch of car wheels on the gravel road leading up to my property. My eyebrows knit together and I walk toward the sound, ready to intercept whoever made the long, winding drive up to talk to me. They're either lost, or something is wrong. I don't get many visitors that come up just for a chat.

The familiar Lang Creek County Police emblem comes into view on the side of a white pickup truck. I stand at the top of my drive and wait for Sheriff Whittaker to stop the car and get out. He raises his arm toward me as he slams the pickup door closed.

"Aiden! How are you!"

"I'm fine, Bill. What brings you all the way up here?"

"Can't a man come and see his friend and make sure everything is all right? I haven't stopped by the garage in a while."

I nod with pursed lips. I don't like being reminded of work, and I spend as little time there as possible.

Bill walks toward me and extends his hand. I grasp it and we pump our arms up and down before he claps me on the back with his other hand.

"Good to see you're still alive, friend."

I nod toward the cabin. "Drink?"

Bill hesitates and points his thumb at his truck. "I haven't got much time today, Aiden. I'm on duty in town. There's actually something I wanted to talk to you about."

I nod slowly. I can feel that empty feeling in the pit of my stomach when I know there is bad news coming. My mind races to my brothers - did anything happen to them? Surely Bill wouldn't be in such a good mood if it did? I stare at him until he nods and opens his mouth to speak.

"There's a town hall meeting this Friday," he starts.

I shake my head. "Not interested." I turn toward the cabin and start walking away from Bill. His footsteps crunch as he jogs toward me.

"Aiden, wait! You've heard of the new hotel, haven't you? They're sending a representative to tell the town about it. We're going to vote on the construction. Your property runs alongside the hotel grounds for at least four acres. If anyone should have a say, it's you."

I stop and turn toward him. "You already know what I think about that hotel, Bill," I growl. Bill nods and takes another step closer to me. He spreads his palms up toward the sky and pleads with his eyes.

"Aiden, the town is divided. I agree with you, I don't think the hotel should be there, but what can I do? I'm the Sheriff, for Christ's sake. I need to be at least somewhat neutral. We need you to speak your mind."

I stare at his eyes and feel myself harden. My body becomes stiff and my gaze gets hard and cold. Bill stands his ground, staring into my face as I feel that familiar current of anger and resentment fill me up. I shake my head and turn back toward the cabin.

"Get one of my brothers to go," I call back. "I'm not interested."

"I can't!" Bill says. "Ethan is gone for Park Ranger training and Dominic... well, you know how Dominic is."

"So all that's left is me, is that it? Last resort?" I ask as I glance over my shoulder. Bill grins and shrugs his shoulders.

"Something like that."

I hesitate. If my brothers can't make it to town, no one will have the courage to speak up against the construction of the hotel. It's endorsed by the McCoy family, and they own half the town. Every time I pull on my coveralls to go to work with 'McCoy Trucking' branded across the chest, I almost shudder with disgust.

If this hotel gets built, the whole county will change. The virgin forest that surrounds us will be destroyed by droves of tourists and the quiet, sleepy town that I've always known will be overrun. My family's property will be the first to be impacted. I can hear my father's voice in my head telling me to go to the meeting. It's my duty to protect these forests.

But then I think about driving into town. I think about seeing Mara McCoy's mother at the town hall meeting and the way she'll look me up and down and lift her lip in a disgusted snarl. I shake my head.

"I'm busy, Bill. Get someone else."

I see Bill's shoulders slump before I turn back toward the cabin. I listen as his footsteps walk away from me toward his truck and hear the truck's motor start. I open the door to the cabin and walk inside without looking back. With a deep breath, I bring my hands up to my face and blow out all the air from my lungs.

I peel my jacket off and toss it toward a chair before kicking my work boots off. It only takes a couple steps before I'm in the kitchen. I rip the refrigerator door open and crack a beer. The cold liquid runs down my throat and by the time I put it back down, half of it is gone. I set the beer on the counter and wipe my lips on the back of my hand. My eyes drift up through the kitchen window. The corner of the big house is just visible through the trees. A pang goes through my heart and I shake my head.

I was supposed to be there, with a wife and kids, living the way my father taught us. I wanted to fill every one of the four bedrooms with children and teach them everything I knew. I wanted to smell warm cooking coming from the luxurious kitchen and know that I had a good woman beside me.

That never happened though.

Mara and her family betrayed us, and now I'm here. I'm living in a tiny cabin working for the family that took everything from my brothers and me.

The small cabin at the back of the property is all I need. I don't need a big house, or a woman, or children. I don't need to be involved in the town's problems. It doesn't matter if they build a hotel or not. It doesn't concern me. I finish my beer in one more gulp and toss the empty bottle into the trash. My eyes drift up toward the big house and I feel a shiver curl up my spine.

What will happen to it when the hotel is built? Will anyone come snooping through these woods? I shake my head. I know they will, and the little slice of peace that I've found up here will be gone forever.

MADELINE

I COLLAPSE onto my sofa when I get to my apartment. I try to turn my brain off, but it's still buzzing with all the things I have to do. I empty my purse and put my work phone and personal phone on the coffee table before slowly getting up to get myself a glass of water. I don't have the energy to make dinner tonight.

I only have three days before I need to leave for Lang Creek, and all three days will be completely packed with work. It seems to be the only thing I ever do anymore.

From the kitchen I hear my phone ring. I know it's my personal phone from the ringtone, and my heart sinks. The only person that would be calling me at this hour is my mother. I amble back to the living room and pick up my phone, sighing one last time before picking up.

"Hi, Mom," I breathe.

"Madeline! I have been trying to get through to you all day!"

"I was at work," I answer, my voice more terse than I mean it to be.

"Are you still doing that? Why don't you come and work for your father, dear? The hours will be much more manageable."

I bristle. We've been through this a million times, and a million times I've told her that I don't want to work for my father. The main reason I went into environmental engineering was to get away from all of the environmental destruction due to the oil and gas industry.

"Did you need anything, mom?" I ask.

"Yes! Pack your bag, you need to stay with us this weekend. Your father's doctor ordered him to go down to warmer weather, and with Bianca's new baby I thought it would be a great excuse to have a family vacation. I've booked a floor at the Ritz in Miami."

I try not to sigh audibly. "I have to work, mom, remember? My job? I'm going out to site this week. I can't cancel it."

My mother's exaggerated sigh comes through the phone. "This JOB! It's taking over your life. If you were just sensible, and..."

"I don't want any handouts – job or money or otherwise. I already live in this ridiculous luxury apartment in the middle of Manhattan that's way too big for me. I *don't* want to work in an industry that destroys the earth."

My mother is silent, and I can imagine the expression on her face. It's probably that perfect mix of outrage and disdain that she carries so well.

"Fine. Your father will be heartbroken," she answers.

"He'll live," I shoot back. I immediately regret my words when I hear a strangled sound come from my mother. With my dad's health declining, it's not the type of phrase that I should be throwing around.

"Sorry," I finally say. "I wish I could come. I really do. I just need to be on site this week."

"Well, alright. Be careful."

The phone clicks and I lean back in the sofa. I let out all the air from my lungs and close my eyes. My hands come up to massage my temples as I try not to let the frustration bubble up inside me.

She's right.

I hate the voice in my head but I can't deny it. She's right. I'm working too much, and Dad is sick. I shouldn't be spending my time in Lang fucking Creek, I should be taking all the time I have to spend with him. I don't know how much longer we'll have together.

Maybe I should have just worked with him all these years. Maybe my pride and independence were misplaced, and I should have been grateful. After all, there are certain opportunities that only come with having a last name like Croft.

I remember being a kid and hating the way other kids at school looked at me. We all came from wealthy families – private school kids usually do – but my father made a name for himself with his extreme wealth. They looked at me with that unmistakable mix of respect and jealousy. I could see it from the time I was old enough to understand what jealousy was, and I vowed to myself that I wouldn't live my life riding on my parent's coattails.

And I haven't. Well, I've gotten myself an education with their help, of course. And my mother insisted on buying this apartment, but apart from that I've kept my father's identity a secret from my coworkers and bosses. To them I'm just Madeline Croft, the environmental engineer. I'm not Madeline Croft, the daughter of the oil and gas tycoon.

I open my eyes and glance over at the shelf. I get up slowly and walk over toward the old picture frame. The four of us – me, my sister Bianca, my father and mother. We're all smiling from ear to ear. The scintillating blue waters and bright white buildings of Santorini, Greece splay out behind us.

I grab the frame and stare at my father's face, brushing it gently with my finger. I was only eleven when we went on that trip, but I remember it like it was yesterday. Dad brought me out on a boat and taught me how to fish and I caught a massive red snapper. I still remember the pride in his eyes when we brought it back to shore. He told me I had a gift, and I'd be successful in whatever I chose to do.

The picture frame goes back on the shelf and I blink back the tears in my eyes. I wonder if he still thinks I'm successful. I wonder if when he said that, he was expecting me to take over the family company. I wonder if now, when he sees me, he still sees that girl with a world of possibilities ahead of her.

Maybe he just sees another engineer working for a big company moving up the ladder all too slowly.

I should be with him. I should be going to Miami, but instead I'm heading off into the wilderness. I sigh and turn away from the photo, shaking my head.

I can't think like this. He still has a long time ahead of him, and I have a long time to be with him. It's just one family trip, and I'm at an important point in my career.

I'm making the right choice by going to Lang Creek. I know I am. Maybe if I keep telling myself that I'll start to believe it.

4

AIDEN

My head is stuck under the hood of my father's old Chevrolet when I hear a car coming up the drive. I sigh. I hope this isn't Bill again.

I put down the wrench in my hand and grab my grease rag to wipe my hands. Turning slowly, I lean against the front of the truck and watch the bend in the driveway for the approaching vehicle. My eyebrows inch upward when instead of seeing the Sheriff's pickup, I see my brother's truck rounding the corner.

He pulls up beside me and kills the engine before hopping out of the pickup. I push myself off the front bumper and walk toward him. The driver's side door swings open and I see Dominic's lumbering body come into view. He grunts and nods his chin down at me.

"Got those parts you asked for," he says, nodding his head toward the truck's flatbed.

"I'll help you unload them," I answer. We walk in silence toward the back of his truck where he opens the gate. I nod in appreciation. "Thanks, Dominic," I say. I've been trying to fix Dad's old Chevy for weeks, and these look like they'll do the trick.

Dominic just grunts in response. I steal a glance his way and think of Bill's words. I'm not surprised he didn't ask Dominic to represent the town in the upcoming meeting. Physically, my brother is imposing. He's even bigger than me and I've always been built like an ox. But he is a man of few words, and the likelihood of him standing in front of a room full of people and voicing an opinion seems almost impossible.

I help Dominic unload the parts and nod in approval when I pick up the alternator.

"Where did you find this?" I ask. "I thought they didn't make these anymore. None of our suppliers at work had any."

Dominic shrugs and drops his load on the work bench in the garage. "Scrap yard," he explains. I nod and check the other things he's brought. A smile plays on my lips and I glance at my brother.

"This should do it. I'll have it up and running within the week," I tell him with a grin.

Dominic nods and starts walking back toward his truck. He pauses when he gets to the door, lifting his eyes up toward me and knitting his eyebrows together.

"You going to that town hall meeting?" he asks.

The question surprises me. It surprises me that he knows about the meeting in the first place, and it surprises me that he'd expect me to go. It's my turn to knit my brows together and I shrug.

"Not my business," I answer. Dominic's gaze hardens and he searches my face. I resist the urge to look away, keeping my gaze steady on my older brother. He used to look at me like this when we were kids, and it took me years to learn to keep eye contact.

"It is because of the McCoys?" he asks. Again, I'm surprised at his words. I don't remember the last time Dominic asked me an open-ended question about something other than cars and home maintenance.

I crack and finally look down at the gravel between us. My eyes search the rocks for an answer and I can feel my brother's gaze boring into me. I shrug.

"It's just not my business. Got nothing to do with them. I work for them, remember? It's not like I'm afraid of running into them."

"Dad wouldn't have wanted it," he says. "The hotel." I glance up at him and see a flash of something in his eyes. It looks almost tender, and then in an instant it's gone. He grunts at me and swings the door open, sliding his massive body behind the steering wheel. I watch him reverse and drive away before letting out a sigh.

I don't know what's inside me – frustration, maybe. Anger, even. Why does it have to be me that represents the town? There has to be someone else in town that can speak up against the new hotel!

As soon as the thought crosses my mind, I know there's no one. No one except us owns as much land as the McCoys. No one else has the weight of generations of family living in the area.

As much as I know it has to be me, I hate the thought of it. I hate the thought of driving into town when it's not absolutely necessary. I hate the thought of seeing those familiar streets and swallowing all the bitter memories that come with it.

I'm happy up here on my own. I don't need anything else. This mountain, these forests - it's all I need. The reason I came up here and the reason I stay up here is to get away from Lang Creek and all its problems. Sure, I took a job at the garage, but I hardly have to drive into town to go there. The McCoy Trucking maintenance yard is on the way into town, so most days I don't even see anyone on my way in.

My eyes drift up toward the empty old house. I can just see the corner of it through the trees. I haven't been up there since I moved out after Dad died and it's almost completely overgrown. The cabin that I live in looks like a shack next to it and I shake my head.

I know that Bill is right. I know that Dominic is right. I have to go to the town hall meeting. I have to fulfill my promise to my father and protect these forests with every ounce of strength that I have.

If not for me, if not for the forest, then I have to do it for the memory of my father. I run my fingers over the car parts, resting my index on the alternator. I pick it up and turn it over in my hand, glancing at the old car I've been working on.

What's the point of restoring this car in memory of my father if I ignore his dying request? What's the point of living up here if I won't try to keep these forests free from development companies who want to clear cut the entire mountainside?

My eyes drift one more time to my childhood home and I nod to myself. I'll go to the town hall meeting. I'll speak my mind and I'll do everything I can to stop this hotel being built. I owe it to this mountain, I owe it to this forest, and I owe it to my father.

5

MADELINE

IT'S ALMOST three hours from the airport over to Lang Creek. I grip the steering wheel in my rental car and navigate the winding roads, going higher and higher up through the mountains. I peer through the windshield at the jaw-dropping scenery that spreads out around me in all directions.

It may be a long drive, but I understand why my company wants to build a hotel here. The mountains are massive and awe-inspiring. After a few hours of head-swiveling and jaw-dropping, I finally see a sign that tells me I'm entering the town of Lang Creek. I slow the car down and glance out the windows, studying the old buildings and small-town charm. I definitely understand why we're building here.

The town is built in a valley between two mountains, with houses spilling up the lower slopes of the peaks. The main street runs directly between the mountains. I see the shop and small existing hotel just ahead.

I pull up outside the hotel and read the sign: McCoy's Hotel. I turn off the engine and take a deep breath.

Tomorrow evening, I'll be facing the townspeople. I'll be telling them exactly what my company wants them to hear. I'll be trying to convince them to support the construction of a multi-million-dollar luxury hotel in the heart of their small town.

My eyes swing around to take in the small timber houses and the handmade signs that line the shopfronts. My lips purse together. A small tendril of something starts to curl inside me.

Is it doubt? I've always thought that I was doing something good for the world as an environmental engineer. I'm on the good guys' side. That's what I always tell myself, anyway.

But now as I look at this little town, nestled between two mountains and surrounded by thick forest, I wonder if I'm doing the right thing.

I shake my head.

I can't think like that. It's just because I didn't want to come here, and I thought I should be with my father instead of in this place. Of course I'm doing the right thing. We're bringing business to the area, jobs, and cash flow. I'm here to make sure that it happens ethically and that the delicate ecosystem of these virgin forests won't be disturbed more than necessary.

Those are all good things. I'm one of the good guys.

I finally open the door and swing my legs out, stretching my arms overhead and cracking my back before grabbing my small suitcase out of the back seat. I take a deep breath and start heading toward McCoy's Hotel. With a bit more preparation tonight and tomorrow, I should be ready for the town hall meeting. I'll be ready to convince the townspeople that they should be happy about this project.

A bell jingles as I walk into the hotel lobby and an older woman looks up from the desk. A smile spreads across her face as she looks at me.

"You must be Madeline Croft," she says. "I've been expecting you. Was the drive okay?"

"The drive was great," I respond. "It's so beautiful over here."

"That's why we want to share it with the world," she answers. She smiles at me again and I can't help but feel like she's smiling a bit too hard. It's almost forced, or it's like the smile doesn't spread all the way to her eyes. She nods at me before shuffling some papers in front of her. The check-in process is quick, and I'm hit with a barrage of information on the area. She tells me what to do, where to go, what to avoid. I nod and try to absorb it all, taking the brochures and maps from her with a smile. She hands me a key and points toward the staircase.

"Just up the stairs to the left. Room number 206."

"Thank you, Mrs. McCoy," I say.

"Please," she says with another forced smile. "Call me Margaret. Ask me if you have any questions whatsoever."

I smile and nod before turning toward the stairs. They creak as I walk up, and I glance down the bright hallway toward the numbers on the doors. Number 206 is the third door down.

It's a clean room, with a cozy quilt and fresh flowers in the vase. I drop my suitcase and let all the air out of my lungs as I look around the room. This is my new home for the next few days. I don't even know how long I'll be here. The way Barry was talking it sounded like it would be a few weeks.

My phone buzzes and I glance down to see a picture message from my mother. I open it up to see the family smiling at a beach resort. My father looks tired and ill and my heart squeezes as I look at the photo. I know that my mother is trying to make me feel guilty for choosing work over this vacation, but I refuse to give in. I need to do this for myself, and I need to pursue my career the way that I want to do it.

I send her a quick message back and tuck my phone away. It's time to get some dinner at the restaurant downstairs, and then one final practice run through my presentation. Tomorrow morning I'm visiting the construction site and meeting with Cecilia and the site team. I glance around the room one more time and take a deep breath. Whether I like it or not, this is my new home.

When I walk downstairs, I glance out the big bay windows at the front of the hotel. The mountain is lit up with the sunset and the sky is ablaze with colors. The tightness in my chest loosens slightly and a smile spreads across my lips.

It might not be a beach vacation in Miami, but it doesn't mean this place isn't gorgeous. Maybe my new home isn't so bad after all.

6

———

AIDEN

MY FATHER'S truck rumbles to life in the driveway. I smile as I run my hands over the steering wheel. I still remember being a young kid bouncing on the passenger seat as my father drove me through the winding mountain roads. Now it's me in the driver's seat, but it still feels like he's here with me.

I glance at my watch and nod to myself. If I leave now, I should make it down to Lang Creek just as the town hall meeting starts. My heart starts beating faster at the thought of driving into town, but I put the truck in gear and start driving before I can change my mind.

The long winding roads are comforting in their familiarity. I drive slowly, taking my time and enjoying the feel of the truck underneath me. I've always loved this vehicle, and it feels great to have it running again. I shift gears as I get to the main road into town and turn toward Lang Creek.

The truck jerks and shudders underneath me. I frown, trying to accelerate. The truck shudders again and starts to slow. I shift gears again and try to get the vehicle moving, but it shakes one more time and completely shuts off. I coast for a few feet before slowing to a stop as I pull over onto the shoulder.

Fuck.

I take a deep breath and pop the hood. I can see some smoke starting to curl up from the motor and I already know I won't be able to fix this without tools. I lift the hood up anyway and cough as a cloud of black smoke billows out toward my face.

I glance back up the road toward my cabin. It's twelve miles away. Lang Creek is three miles down the road. As much as I hate the thought of walking to town and asking for help, it's the only chance I have of getting this truck off the road tonight. And of course, just my luck, everyone will be at that town hall meeting to hear about it.

The hood slams shut and I take a deep breath, filling my lungs with cool mountain air before heading off toward Lang Creek. Every step makes my heart beat a little bit harder. I'm not sure I'll be able to speak up in front of everyone, in front of Margaret McCoy, in front of all the people who know what happened between our families. Even though I know why I need to speak up, I still wish someone else would do it.

By the time I walk onto Main Street, the sweat is beading on my forehead and I've opened my jacket up to let the air cool my body. I can feel a droplet of sweat running down my spine and I wipe my forehead with my sleeve. I check my watch and curse under my breath. Not only am I going to be late, I'm going to burst in dripping with sweat and asking for a lift back up to my cabin.

It's not exactly the image of a strong opposition. I can almost hear the townspeople sniggering under their breath as I walk in asking for their help. I haven't asked for help in years.

When I was a kid, my father was respected in the town. People looked to him for advice and guidance for everything from car maintenance to mountain safety. He built most of the houses in town himself, and was almost the unofficial mayor of the town. When he died, it's like the whole town became fragmented. No one knew who to turn to for help, and the whole rhythm of life was disrupted.

Maybe that was just my fourteen-year-old perspective of it. My father, the superhero, was taken before his time. My boots stomp on the ground as I make my way toward Lang Creek. If it were up to me, I'd be heading in the opposite direction, moving away from all the memories that assault me whenever I go into town. If it were up to me, my father would still be alive and my brothers and I would speak to each other more.

If it were up to me, maybe I wouldn't be alone on that mountain all the time.

I shake my head to dispel the thought. I like being alone. I like working by myself, and hearing the noises of the forest as I fall asleep. I like living on the mountain and seeing its beauty everywhere I turn. I like using my hands and feeling the cool air burn my lungs when I'm working hard outside. I like heading into my tiny cabin and sleeping in my single bed as if I were a hibernating bear.

I know that I like all these things, but as my steps take me closer and closer to the Lang Creek town hall meeting, I can't help but wonder how convincing I'll be. I know what I could say to oppose the construction of this hotel. I'd talk about my father's legacy, about protecting the mountains and worshipping their power over us. I'd talk about the thousands of birds and insects and animals that call these forests home. I'd talk about the plants that feed us and protect us from the harshness of the winters.

I'd talk about all those things, but right now, all I can think about is speaking up and seeing all the eyes telling me that I've failed my father. Whenever I see the McCoys, all I can think of is how they betrayed my father. Every day when I go to work at their maintenance yard, it's like rubbing salt in the wound.

I'm not the man that my father was, or at least they don't think I am.

My heart squeezes just as I pass the huge wooden sign that says, 'Welcome to Lang Creek'. My father put up that sign. I used to feel pride every time we'd drive into town. Now all I feel is pain.

I can already see the lights in Town Hall. The meeting must be underway already. I take a deep breath and force myself to speed up.

It doesn't matter what Margaret McCoy says, or what her daughter Mara did to my family. It doesn't matter that my father's gone, or that my brothers and I hardly speak anymore. All that matters is that this hotel will destroy everything my family believed in for generations. It'll destroy the sanctity of the mountains and make it impossible for life to go on as it has.

Those words are on repeat, playing over and over in my head until my jaw is set and my chin dips downwards. I plant my palm against the door and push it open, letting the warmth of the indoors wash over me. Voices filter through to me from the main hall, and I square my shoulders before heading in that direction.

Before I turn the last corner, I hear a voice I've never heard before. It's sweet and melodic, and it makes my heart jump in my chest. My eyebrows knit together as I try to recognize it. With every step that takes me closer to the voice, my heart starts thumping a little bit harder. I can't even make out the words. Something about conservation, or the environment.

I turn the final corner and see the main hall – it takes all my self-control to stop my jaw from dropping. When I heard the project's environmental engineer would come to speak at the meeting, I was expecting to see an old man with a big potbelly, or maybe a young man with a big ego.

I wasn't expecting a woman.

I wasn't expecting a woman *like her*.

Her rich, brown hair is pulled back into a low bun, with wisps of it framing her face. She's got high cheekbones and full pink lips. From the back of the room, I can't tell what color her eyes are. She's standing with her shoulders back and her head held high as she flicks through a couple slides of her presentation.

The door slams behind me and I jump as the whole room turns toward the noise. The woman's eyes lift up toward me and for a brief instant we look at each other. Time stops, and the room is empty except for her and me.

I forget why I'm here, or what I'm supposed to say. I forget everything except the fact that she's the most beautiful woman that I've ever seen.

7

MADELINE

I STUMBLE over my words when the door slams. I stop in the middle of a sentence and it takes me a few moments to remember what I was saying. I've never seen anyone like him before. His body seems to take up the entire width of the door, and even from the front of the room I can sense the fresh forest air that surrounds him.

His eyes look black from here. His beard is full and he stands completely still as he stares at me. My heart is thumping and I forget to breathe until Cecilia clears her throat beside me. I snap out of my stupor.

"...and the stringent conservation practices that have been displayed thus far in the project will continue for the full duration. As mentioned, a percentage of the hotel's profits will go toward the maintenance of the National Park."

I flick to the next slide and try to avoid looking at the man. It's almost like I can sense his every movement. I know that he moves to the left and takes the first available seat. I know that he nods at the sheriff, and I know that he keeps his eyes locked on me.

I know that the space between my thighs is pulsing, and my cheeks are burning even when I'm not looking in his direction. I know that I want to learn his name, and I want to smell his chest and feel his body against mine.

With a shake of my head, I finish my presentation and hand it over to Cecilia. She continues to speak and it takes all my self-control to keep my eyes from wandering toward the stranger at the back of the room.

I can't do it. I have to give in. I flick my eyes toward him and feel the heat in my core increase when I see he's looking straight at me. I don't hear Cecilia or the questions from the crowd or anything else for the next few minutes. All I hear is my own heartbeat in my ears and all I see is the stranger's broad shoulders and his dark eyes staring straight at me.

"Madeline?" Cecilia says, eyes wide as she stares at me. I whip my head toward her and she gives me a loaded look. "The gentleman in the green shirt was wondering what we were going to do about the waste produced by the hotel."

I jump up off my seat and grab the microphone from her, putting on my most professional face. I turn to the man who asked the question and answer as best I can, saying exactly what I've been trained to say. His lips purse as I speak and his eyebrows come together, and I know that I haven't convinced him.

My heart jumps when the man in the back stands up. He stalks toward the podium in the center aisle and the man in the green shirt steps aside. A hush falls over the room as everyone waits for him to speak. My heart is thumping against my ribcage and I try my hardest to keep my gaze steady on him.

Be professional. Be professional. Be professional.

He finally opens his mouth to speak and I hear the smooth baritone notes of his voice. It sends a thrill through my whole body to hear his voice's rich depth. I'm so focused on listening to him speak that I almost don't hear what he says.

"... and these forests have been protected for generations. Nothing that you have said today guarantees the conservation of the forest and its inhabitants. In fact, the increase in tourism will do nothing but destroy the mountains that we have come to love and respect. It's people like you," he says, lifting a hand to point directly at me. "People like you who come from the city and try to tell us what to think. We don't care about your profits, or your jobs, or your money. We care about the mountains and we care about this town. Build your hotel elsewhere."

The room erupts in applause. The man in the green shirt stands up to clap the stranger on the back. Now that he's close, I can see that his eyes are dark, almost black. They're burning with anger and right now the full force of it is directed at me. I take a step back before squaring my shoulders and clenching my jaw. He won't make me back down so easily.

"Mr... I'm sorry I didn't catch your name," I start.

"Clarke."

"Mr. Clarke," I continue. "I understand your reservations. I can assure you that every precaution will be taken to – "

"Your precautions don't mean shit," he interrupts. I can feel my spine stiffening, and the pulsing between my legs dies down as the anger builds inside me. "All you care about is the bottom line. You can show us these fancy presentations and graphs and figures but it means fuck all."

Before I can answer, Margaret, the hotel owner, jumps up from her seat.

"That's enough, Aiden. You have no right to waltz back into town and say this kind of thing when you've done nothing but live on your own up in the mountains. If it wasn't for MY garage, you probably wouldn't even care if this town existed. You have no idea what this town has been through over the past couple years. This hotel is our ticket to new industry, new people, to new *life*."

Aiden's face darkens as he turns toward Margaret. His lip curls upwards into a snarl and my heart jumps in my chest as I wait to hear him speak.

Before he can say anything, Sheriff Whittaker takes a step forward.

"That's enough now. Margaret, Aiden, sit down." He speaks with authority, and after a few tense seconds, both of them back down. I watch as Aiden stalks toward the back of the room and walks straight out the door. When it slams shut behind him, my shoulders slump and I feel like the breath has left my body.

The rest of the meeting is a blur. Before I know it, the townspeople are filtering out and I'm gathering my things. Cecilia says something to me and I answer, not knowing what either of us say. When I get back to the hotel, Margaret McCoy congratulates me on my presentation and all I can do is grunt in response.

There's only one thing on my mind, and it isn't the presentation. It isn't the hotel, or construction, or engineering. It's *him*. All I can think of is the way his body seemed to fill the whole room, and the way his eyes pierced through me.

Aiden Clarke.

I know his name, but I need to find out who he is. I need to see him again.

8

AIDEN

My mind is a hurricane. I hear the door slam behind me and I stomp toward the exit. I don't know where I'm going or what I'm doing, I just know I need to get out of here.

I need to get away from the McCoys. I need to get away from that woman. I need to get away from Bill and everyone who was relying on me to oppose the construction of this hotel.

I can't do it. If my truck was here, I'd be straight in it and on my way back up to the safety of my cabin. Instead, I open the doors and let the cool air wash over me. I close my eyes and take a deep breath, letting the fresh mountain air fill my lungs and calm down my burning anger.

A truck pulls up in front of the town hall and my brother Dominic gets out. I nod to him and he dips his chin down in response.

"How'd it go?" he asks, looking toward the building behind me.

"About as well as expected," I respond. I see a hint of a grin on Dominic's face.

"Saw your truck on the road. You need a ride?"

"Yeah, thanks," I reply. It's times like these that I'm glad Dominic doesn't say much. I get into the passenger seat and we drive all the way back to the cabin in silence. When we pass my truck, Dominic says he'll bring me back down to it tomorrow and help me fix it. Apart from that, I have the entire drive back to mull over the evening.

My thoughts flick between Margaret McCoy's weasel-like face and the beautiful dark-haired engineer. I don't know what to make of her. She seemed so sincere, like she really believed what she was saying about the conservation and sustainability of the hotel.

Maybe she's just naive, and she thinks those things are true. Maybe she hasn't seen the destruction that goes with big construction projects, or the degradation of nature that happens when tourists are left to run amuck. Either way, I want to believe her, but I just can't.

Dominic pulls the truck up in front of the cabin and turns toward me.

"You think this hotel is going to go ahead?" he asks. I turn toward him and we stare at each other for a few moments. I take a deep breath and shrug.

"What can we do? With Dad gone, the McCoys basically hold all the sway in town. A lot of people agreed with me, but that doesn't really mean much compared to the money and control they have."

Dominic grunts in response and shifts his gaze forward. He nods to the big house.

"You been in there lately?"

I follow his gaze and look at the corner of our childhood home. I shake my head and try to speak, but it comes out as a croak. My throat tightens as I look at the old building.

"Nah," I say. "Not in a long time."

Dominic nods, and I take that as a goodbye. I slip out the car and wave as he drives back down the mountain. My cabin is cold and dark when I go inside, and I spend the next few minutes ignoring my thoughts and starting a fire in the wood stove.

Once it's lit, I sit down and watch the flames as they dance in front of me. I close my eyes and lean back, letting the warmth seep into my bones. It doesn't take long for the whole cabin to heat up, and the familiar smell of burning wood fills the room.

The woman's face paints itself on my eyelids. I don't even know her name. All I know is that she's an environmental engineer. When I got closer, I could see that her eyes were a pale brown, and her lips were a deep, pink color. It's hard to remember what I said, or what she said, or what anyone said. All I could focus on was the heaviness of my cock between my legs and the way her eyes flicked up toward me every few minutes.

I didn't want to yell at her. I didn't want to tell her to stop the construction of the hotel. I didn't want to be applauded by opposing everything she stood for.

All I wanted was for her to see me.

I open my eyes again and watch the flames through the glass door in the wood stove, trying to figure out these feelings. For years, all I've wanted was to be alone up here. Being in my cabin by myself, living off the land and spending as much time in the mountains as possible. That's what has made me happy.

At least, I think this is happiness.

The alternative is to get to know someone else – only to have my heart shattered into a billion pieces again, just like Mara McCoy did to it all those years ago. I don't want to feel like that. I don't want to be the laughingstock of the town. I definitely don't want to get involved with some woman from the city who's intent on ruining the mountains with a big fancy hotel.

The restlessness inside me bubbles up and I grab a flashlight from the shelf. I rip the cabin door open and head up toward the big house. The weak beam of light saves me from tripping on overgrown tree roots and bushes as I make my way up to my childhood home. The rickety old steps are rotting, and I step on them carefully. They groan under my weight as I make my way toward the door.

The front door isn't even locked. I push it open and peer through the opening. It looks like a time capsule, left exactly how it was when my brothers and I moved out. I've lived a few feet away from this house and for years I haven't bothered to come up here.

The flashlight beam illuminates the house I grew up in. I walk through the rooms one by one until I get to my old bedroom. I find a picture of my seventh birthday, when my parents had taken the three of us boys up to the top of the mountain. It was the first time I'd summited a mountain that big, and in the picture my whole face is beaming with pride. My father's hand is on my shoulder, and my mother is holding a cupcake that she carried all the way up just for me.

It was the perfect birthday. We were together, we were happy, and we were on top of the world. It was before Mom died of cancer the next year, and before the ordeal with Dad and the McCoys a few years later. It was before my whole world got turned upside down. I slip the photo into my pocket and turn around, trying to ignore the prickling in my eyes and the tightness in my chest. I hurry out of the house, making sure to lock the front door as I leave.

When I walk back to the cabin, I don't look back. I sit down in my chair by the fire and take the photo out of my pocket, propping it up on the side table beside me. I glance at it once more before turning back to the fire, feeling the ice in my heart melt ever so slightly as I sit in the warmth of my tiny mountain cabin.

9

———

MADELINE

"Barry, I have all those applications to submit! I can't stay here!"

"Cecilia said she needed help. Based on your report from the town hall meeting it sounds like she's right. You can finish the applications from there. Consider yourself mobilized to site."

"You told me this would be temporary, and I'd be back in New York by the end of next week. I don't even have any clothes with me!"

Barry sighs on the other side of the line. "Get them packed up by a friend and we'll pay to ship them to you," he answers. "You need to stay until this mess is sorted out."

"It's not a mess, Barry. Cecilia has it under control. Her community garden idea is getting a lot of positive support from the townspeople."

"We're going to need more than a community garden, Maddy. You know that," he answers a little more gently. I take a deep breath and nod.

"Fine. But you owe me. And I'm expecting an extra allowance for working away from home for this. And a raise."

"I knew I could count on you," he responds. I can hear the smile in his voice. "Send through those applications when they're ready and I'll review them as soon as I can."

We hang up the phone and I stare at my computer screen, not knowing what to think. I'm sitting in my tiny hotel room, with my laptop wedged on the console table with hardly any room for paperwork. The site offices aren't ready yet, so this is what I have to work with. I run my hand over my forehead and shake my head from side to side. I need some air.

I grab a jacket and head out for a walk. When I get to the lobby, I breathe a sigh of relief when I see that Mrs. McCoy isn't at the front desk. I slip out the door and pick a direction to walk in, letting my feet take me wherever they'll go.

The air is brisk, and I look up toward the mountain peaks that are visible all around me. My heartbeat slows and I feel my shoulders relax, as if the mountains around me are soothing me with their presence. I walk down the main road until the buildings become more sparse and the pine trees become more dense. The road's shoulder is wide enough to walk on, so I just wander until my mind is clear and the only noise I hear is my breath and my own footsteps.

I don't know how long I've been walking when I spot something in the distance. There are two cars parked on the shoulder in front of me. I can see two men looking under the hood of the closest car and I speed up slightly to see what's going on.

It's not until I'm too close to turn around that I recognize the man from last night's meeting - Aiden Clarke. He looks up just as I realize it's him. His gaze hardens and he squares his shoulders toward me. I slow to a stop and the other man turns toward me. I glance at him, frowning slightly when I see the same dark eyes and strong jaw looking back at me. They must be brothers.

I clear my throat. "Hi," I say simply.

"Hi," Aiden responds. He glances at his brother and then back at me.

"You having car troubles?" I ask, nodding to his car. He grunts and I silently curse myself for my stupid question. Obviously, he's having car troubles. "My name is Madeline, by the way. You can call me Maddy."

"Aiden," he growls. "This is Dominic."

Dominic nods at me and I nod back. I shift my weight from foot to foot, trying to think of something to say. Aiden's dark eyes are still boring into me and I try to ignore the spark igniting between my legs. Aiden nods to the pickup behind his.

"You mind grabbing the wrench from the back of the truck over there?"

"Sure," I say right away, glad to have an excuse to avoid his gaze. I shuffle toward the other vehicle and find the wrench in the back of the pickup. I bring it back and hand it to Aiden, who takes it with a nod. I watch as he and his brother work side by side without a word, as if they've been doing it all their lives.

"Aiden," I hesitate. "I just wanted to say that I heard what you said yesterday, and I want you to know that -"

"Wanted me to know what?" He interrupts, turning toward me. His eyes are blazing and I take a step back. I don't know if the beating in my heart is from the look in his eyes or the musky smell that's making my head spin.

"I...I just want to reassure you that your concerns were heard. We're doing everything we can to preserve the natural beauty of the area."

"Do you actually believe that?" he asks. His voice is softer, but his eyes are still burning with the same intensity. "Do you actually believe that the company you work for gives a rat's ass about these mountains?"

My heart is thumping. I'm trying my hardest to ignore the urge to reach out and touch his chest. I nod my head and swallow.

"Yes," I answer. "I do believe that."

Dominic snorts and Aiden shakes his head. "You must be new to this industry then," he says, turning back toward his truck. "Because all they care about is dollars and cents."

My heart is thumping and I open my mouth, but I can't think of anything to say. I desperately want him to look at me again. I want to see that fire in his eyes, and I want to know what he means. I want to see what he sees when he looks at the mountains, and I want to understand why he's so worried about the construction of the hotel.

I want to know what he thinks, and why he thinks it.

I want to know all these things, but all I can do is nod slowly and turn back toward the town. I take a few steps before turning back toward the two brothers.

"We're building a community garden," I say. It feels silly to say it, but I keep talking. "We're starting next week. Down near the church, on 2nd Street. It would be a great to have you help."

Aiden stops moving and turns his head. I can see his profile as he chews on my words. All he does is grunt in response before turning back toward his truck's motor. My heart sinks ever so slightly and I let my feet take me back toward Lang Creek.

10

—————

AIDEN

"WHAT?" I say, maybe a bit too aggressively. Dominic shrugs. His eyebrow is raised and I see the hint of a smile on his face.

"Nothing," he replies, turning back to the motor. He nods once. "Should work now. Give it a try."

Grateful to be away from his teasing look, I slide into the driver's seat and turn the key in the ignition. My father's old truck rumbles to life and Dominic drops the hood back down. He nods at me through the windshield before circling over to the driver's side window. I roll it down and he pokes his head through.

"Maybe you should check out this community garden," he says in his signature gruff voice. His words surprise me, and I'm not quite sure how to respond.

"Why?" I ask. I know my voice is hard and challenging, but Dominic doesn't flinch. He just shrugs.

"Think she likes you," he says. The grin is back, and I feel my cheeks redden. My brother taps the door of the truck and nods once before walking back toward his own truck. I watch him get into it in the rear-view mirror and then glance forward toward town, in the direction that Madeline disappeared. I shake my head and swing the car around back toward my lonely cabin in the mountains.

The whole ride back, I think of Madeline. Maddy. She stood in front of me, shifting her weight from side to side. She tucked her hair behind her ear and looked at me through her eyelashes in a way that made my cock twitch. Even the thought of it now makes it throb between my legs.

I shift in my seat and try to focus on the road.

She's the enemy.

I need to remember that. No matter how pretty or sexy or charming she is, she represents everything that my father and my brothers stand against. She represents development and the destruction of these forests that we call home.

Still, the thought of seeing her again makes my heart beat a little bit faster. I know I shouldn't. I know I should keep my distance, but I can't help but think about going to help with the community garden project. Maybe it would help me integrate back into the town. Maybe if I start spending more time down there, the McCoy's hold on everyone will loosen and we'll be able to oppose them on this hotel thing.

I snort as the thoughts pass through my head. The only reason I'd be going down there would be to see Maddy. I wouldn't care about Lang Creek or the McCoys or my father's legacy. All I'm thinking of is the weight of my cock and how sensitive it feels as it rubs against my legs.

When I get in front of the cabin, I kill the engine and swing my legs out of the truck. My footsteps crunch on the gravel as I make my way toward my cabin. I look around and shake my head. What would she think if she came here? She'd think I'm completely feral.

Maybe I am.

I've gone wild since Dad died, since my brothers moved away and Mara McCoy broke my heart. I don't go into town, and I stay in this tiny cabin I call home. I walk to the back of the cabin to the outdoor shower and turn it on full blast. The water heats up and steam starts billowing as I peel my clothes off my body. Working on the engine made me sweat, and my clothes are stuck to me. I strip off my jacket, my undershirt, and unbuckle my belt to let my pants puddle at my feet.

When I step under the hot stream of water, I close my eyes and tilt my head back to let the water wash me clean. I stand there for a few seconds, or minutes, or an eternity. I'm not sure how much time passes before I start moving my hand toward my cock. The water is running down it and dripping off the tip as it starts to get harder.

I know what's making it hard. It's *her*.

All I can see is the way she stood in front of the townspeople at the town hall meeting, and the way her tight pencil skirt left nothing to the imagination. I close my eyes and wrap my fingers around my cock, feeling it get thicker and harder as my hand moves up and down my shaft.

I'd pull that pencil skirt up so it bunched around her waist and I'd ram my cock inside her. I groan as I pump my cock in my hand, thinking of how tight her body would feel as her walls gripped down on me. My other hand goes up to rest against the wall of the shower and the water runs down over my head as I pull my cock until it's harder than I've felt it in years.

Her skirt would be bunched around her waist and I'd reach back to slap her ass. I can almost hear the sharp crack of skin-on-skin and I can almost see the red handprint of my fingers on her lily white ass. I groan as I think of my hips slamming against her as my cock drives deeper and deeper inside her.

I'd give anything to pump my seed deep inside her. The thought of coming in her and watching it drip out makes my whole body tense and my balls squeeze up toward my body. My orgasm explodes and I grunt as I let my body shudder and tremble, gripping the wall of the shower as the water drips down my entire body.

I'm panting. I finally open my eyes and stand up a bit straighter, moving my head out of the stream of water and taking a few deep breaths. Slowly, methodically, I reach for the soap and start washing myself clean.

I know I shouldn't have done that. I know I should be keeping my distance and keeping her out of my mind. But still, I haven't had an orgasm like that in years. As I wash myself clean, my whole body feels more sensitive than before. I wonder what it would feel like to be inside her. If the thought of her makes me explode like that, what would it feel like to have her skin against mine, and to sink my fingers into her? What would it feel like to run my tongue up and down her slit, and slide my fingers inside her?

I finish washing myself and turn off the shower, taking a deep breath and turning toward the back of the shower wall.

"Fuck," I say under my breath, as I see the empty hook where I keep my towel. I must have left it inside. I gather my dirty clothing and start walking around to the front of the cabin. I'm still imagining Maddy's body and I don't notice the car in the driveway. I don't notice her standing at my front door with her hand raised to knock until she sees me around the corner and yelps.

Our eyes meet for an instant before her gaze drops to take in my nakedness. Her cheeks redden and my cock gets instantly hard. I move my bundle of clothes to cover myself as she looks at the ground beside me.

"Sorry! I'm sorry! I..."

"It's okay. One sec," I say, shuffling by her and opening the door. I slip inside and close the door behind me, my heart thumping against my ribcage as I look down at my naked body. My face flushes as I think about what I was just doing. She'd be a lot more embarrassed if she knew I'd just had the best orgasm I've had in years thinking of her.

11

MADELINE

He goes inside and I rush back to my car. My heart is thumping. I don't know what to do. I just came up here to ask him once again to help with our community garden. I wasn't expecting to see him completely naked, walking around outside like some kind of Tarzan.

Actually, I'm not sure why I came up here. I've been telling myself it's for the project, but now that I'm here – I don't know. I think I just wanted to see him again. I wanted to have his eyes on me, and I wanted to see his broad shoulders and his muscular arms.

I've seen them now, and much more. I grab the car door handle and pull it open. My cheeks are burning and my heart is bouncing against my ribcage. I take a deep breath, trying to ignore the image that's been burned into my mind.

His chiseled, muscular body turned the corner and all I could see was that thick cock swinging between his legs. His abdominal muscles seemed to funnel my gaze straight down to his shaft and the wetness immediately started pooling between my legs.

As I stand next to my car, I close my eyes and enjoy the pulsing of my center for just a second. I haven't felt this turned on in years. I take a deep breath and shake my head.

This is wrong.

Everything is wrong. I shouldn't be here. I shouldn't be imagining him naked. I shouldn't have *seen* him naked! I put a foot into the car and start climbing in when the front door opens and he reappears.

He's wearing pants now, if nothing else. His shoulders are broad and defined, and I can still see that 'v' shape of his abdominals that seems to be pointing to the girth between his legs. My cheeks start to burn again and I look away.

"I'm sorry," I say. "I should go."

"No!" he exclaims, taking a step toward me. He runs his fingers through his hair and bites his lip. My heart does a flip and the wetness between my legs seeps through my panties.

I want him.

I shake my head and grab a brochure from the passenger seat of my car.

"I was just going to bring you this. I know that you're worried about the hotel and how it'll impact your property. I want you to know that I've heard your concerns."

He takes the brochure without looking at it. His eyes are glued on mine and it takes all my self-control to not let my eyes wander down to his bare chest. My hands are itching to reach toward him, to touch his skin and smell his musk.

I shake my head slightly and shrug.

"Anyway, I should be getting back," I mumble, starting to climb back into my car.

"Can I show you something?" he asks. His voice is soft and his eyes seem to plead with me. I hesitate. I'm torn. Part of me just wants to stay near him, to hear his voice and look at his body. Every time his eyes pass over my body it sends a thrill through me. I shouldn't. I know I shouldn't. I open my mouth to give some excuse when he holds up his hand.

"Let me grab a shirt. Stay here."

Usually I'd be offended at being ordered around like that, but I do exactly as he says. My feet stayed rooted to the ground and my hand stays glued on top of the car door as I watch him jog back to his cabin and re-emerge, pulling on a t-shirt. His head pops through and he grins at me. His hair is disheveled and his eyes have a lightness to them when he looks at me.

He runs his fingers through his hair again and nods to a path next to the cabin.

"Come on," he says.

My feet carry me toward him. We walk side by side on the pathway until it becomes too narrow, and then he leads the way. We walk in silence, and I watch the way his ass curves with every step. He pushes branches out of the way, careful to lift them for me as I pass under them. He smiles at me and my heart jumps in my chest. We continue like that for an unknown amount of time, winding our way up the mountain.

The path switches back and forth until the trees thin and we get to a viewpoint. Aiden stops and turns toward me, extending his hand to help me climb a big boulder on the edge. I shake my head.

"I'll stay here," I say, peering over the edge. "I'm fine."

He grins and extends his hand again. "Come on."

I slip my fingers into his and an electric thrill passes through my arm, all the way down to my core. The apex of my thighs is still pulsing and I can feel the wetness of my panties with every step. He pulls me up beside him and we stand on the boulder, overlooking the wide expanse of the Adirondack Mountains below us. I'm hyper aware of his body next to mine as we stand close to each other. It takes me a few moments to take in anything except his presence. When my eyes do sweep over the view, it steals what's left of my breath away.

"Wow," I breathe. "It feels like we're on top of the world."

Aiden doesn't answer. Instead, he points to a bird gliding through the sky. "Peregrine falcon," he says. "There's only a handful of them in these mountains."

He turns to the left and points down the mountainside. "That river has no less than three endangered fish species."

I look at the river he's pointing to, and my gaze travels up to the wide swath of land that's been cleared for the hotel. I feel a lump in my throat and I try to swallow.

"The hotel..."

"They won't survive," he says. "No matter how much sediment protection, how much water treatment, how many signs and warnings and fees you impose on tourists, it won't matter." He turns to face me and I see a deep sadness in his eyes. "This is why the people of Lang Creek don't want this hotel. Don't take it personally."

I still can't speak, and I let my eyes travel along the mountain peaks that surround me. I take a deep breath and let the air fill my lungs. I wonder if I've ever breathed air this fresh. I glance back at Aiden and take a deep breath.

"I don't know what to say," I tell him. His eyes travel up toward me and his lips purse together in a thin line.

"I can't tell you what to do," he says.

With that, he turns back toward the path and holds out his hand. The same thrill passes through my body when our palms touch, and I feel just a little bit emptier when his hand slips out of mine. We walk back down in silence until his cabin comes into view. When we get to my car, we stand in front of each other until I look at his face.

"I know I can't convince you," I say. "But you obviously know these mountains better than anyone else. Won't you come help with the community garden and you can teach me what my company doesn't know? I can help. I can make a difference."

His face sours and he glances into the forest. His eyes swing back toward me and we stay motionless for a few long moments. Finally his chin dips down a fraction of an inch.

"I'll think about it," he says. Without another word, he spins around and stalks back toward his cabin. The door closes behind him and my shoulders slump. I get into my car and drive back down toward Lang Creek, trying to ignore the pulsing between my legs and the fire in my belly.

12

———

AIDEN

I SLUMP DOWN onto the couch and wait for the noise of her car to disappear down the mountain. I close my eyes and rub my temples with my fingers.

She wants me to help. She wants to learn.

Every part of my body wants to be nearer to her. Every part of me wants to feel her skin against mine, to hold her hand and pull her close, but my mind is screaming *no*.

How can I teach her anything when she's powerless to change things? She works for the corporation that's going to destroy our little slice of heaven on these mountains. As good as her intentions are, she doesn't understand that the changes the hotel brings will be irreversible.

I glance toward the shelf and see the picture I brought from the big house. My father's eyes stare back at me from the grave and I get up to slam the picture down. I can't look at him, not now. Not when I'm considering working with Maddy, working with the people who want to destroy my home.

A paper crunches in my pocket and I pull out the brochure that Maddy handed to me. I open it up, looking at the fake rendered photos of the luxury hotel, and I read through the meaningless words that brag about 'sustainability' and 'conservation'. I snort as I read through it and shake my head. I slip the brochure into the stove and watch it curl and disintegrate as it burns.

It's the same bullshit. They say all these things but all they care about are the thousands of tourists that will pay hundreds of dollars a night. They'll walk through these mountains and leave behind trash, trampled ground, and destruction. I watch the brochure burn into nothing and slump down on the sofa.

I SPEND a restless night tossing and turning in my bed. Tonight it feels too hard, or too lumpy, or too cold. I can't get comfortable. Usually when I spend the day outside, working on my car or walking through the forest, I sleep like a log. I fall asleep when the sun goes down and I wake up when it comes up.

Not tonight, though. I wake up when it's still dark out and stare at the ceiling until it becomes too much. Yesterday's events run through my head over and over. I can see the look on Maddy's face when she watched the falcon flying overhead, and how earnest she was about the community garden.

Finally, I swing my legs over the side of the bed and shuffle to the kitchen. I put on a pot of strong coffee and watch it as it brews, trying to ignore the throbbing cock between my legs.

A woman hasn't had this effect on me in years. I can't get her out of my head. When the coffee is ready, I pour the black liquid into a mug and take a long sip. I close my eyes and let the bitter taste fill my mouth, all the while imagining how sweet Maddy's lips would taste if she were here this morning.

I turn around and lean against the counter. I take another sip and head toward the wood-burning stove to start today's fire. There's one colorful piece of paper in there. It's a small corner of the brochure she gave me, a tiny bit of paper that survived the flames. I stare at it and it feels like it's taunting me.

Come into town, it's saying. *Work on the community garden*, it calls out. *See her one more time.*

I take a deep breath. I already know I've lost. Before I know it, I'm showering and getting dressed and heading to my father's old truck. I load up the back of the flatbed with bags of compost I've made at the cabin and take some young plants from my vegetable garden. I load up a spade and a shovel and take a deep breath before closing up the truck.

What am I doing? By showing up to this garden, I'm essentially supporting the construction of the hotel. I shake my head and walk over to the driver's side.

That's not true. I'm going in to see what it's about. The garden will be a good addition to the town, and maybe I can speak to Maddy and teach her more about the area. I can show her that the hotel will only lead to the destruction of these mountains and forests. She's gotten a small taste of them now. She might understand why we care about them so much.

The drive into town is quiet. The early morning mist is lifting as I pass the old timber sign that says, 'Welcome to Lang Creek'. I can feel the pulse through my whole body, and I don't know if it's because I'm in the town that has caused me so much pain, passing the McCoy's hotel, or if it's because I'm going to see Maddy soon.

I turn the corner at the end of town and find the small plot of land set aside for the community garden. No one is here yet, and I check my watch. It's barely past 7am. On a Sunday morning, most people will be in bed for a couple more hours.

I jump out of the truck and start unloading my tools. It looks like there have been some garden plots laid out, but they're in dire need of some good soil and more plants. I look around, still seeing no one, and get to work on my own.

It feels like the old days, when I'd drive into town with my brothers and father and work on various jobs. He'd take us along from the time we were old enough to hold a hammer and taught us how to fix anything that was worth fixing. I work slowly and methodically, from one end of the garden to another, until all the garden plots are freshly turned and ready for planting.

I head toward my truck to grab some rich compost when I hear a whistle. I turn to see Maddy with a grin on her face and an eyebrow raised, looking over the garden with an approving eye.

"I wasn't expecting to see this this morning," she says with a smile. I turn to look at my work and then shrug.

"It's good for the town," I say. "It doesn't mean I think the hotel should be built."

"So you're just using my company, is that it?"

"Something like that," I reply, trying to stifle a grin. "Just like your company is using this town." I can feel the blood pumping through my veins as she takes a step toward me.

Her hair is pulled back in a high ponytail, showing off her gorgeous hazel eyes and her high cheekbones. Her lips look more kissable than ever.

She walks up beside me to grab a bag of compost from my truck. Her arm brushes against mine and my cock twitches in my pants. I think of my shower yesterday, and all I want to do is bend her over the back of the truck and ram my cock into her. She glances up at me and winks before hauling a bag of compost toward the garden.

"Well don't just stand there," she says with a laugh. "Come and help me."

13

MADELINE

It's hard to keep my cool when he's so close. I don't know how long ago he got here, but he's prepped almost the entire garden for planting. We work silently side by side, exchanging furtive glances and blushing without saying anything.

Why is my heart thumping so much? Why does the movement of his body make my center heat up? Why does it feel like an electric thrill passing through my veins every time he looks at me?

I know he's still against the construction of the hotel, and I'm not sure why he's here. He cares about this town and he cares about the mountains, so maybe he was telling the truth when he said that he wanted to do anything that was good for the community.

But every time he looks at me, I can't help but feel like there's something more. He's turning the earth on one of the plots when I walk up with some young plants. We exchange a long glance and he nods to a small hole in the earth.

"Put it in here," he says. I drop the plant in the hole and the two of us pat the rich brown earth gently around the plant. Our soil-covered hands brush against each other and for a moment his fingers intertwine with mine. My heart starts thumping against my ribcage and I look up to see him staring at me. His lips look impossibly soft and my whole body is buzzing with desire.

We leave our hands there, covered in dirt, gently brushing against each other as our eyes devour each other. His shoulders are straining against the fabric of his shirt, and his sweat has soaked through the front in a small 'v'. My eyes trail down and I wish I could see the muscles underneath his shirt ripple and move. I wish I could see his cock again. I'd take it in my hands to feel the smooth hardness of it.

I flick my eyes back up to his and try to swallow. I try to think of something else, but with our fingers intertwined in the dark earth, all I can think about kissing his lips and wrapping my body around his. The seconds tick by and he tilts his head toward me. I can smell the piney musk of his body as he gets closer. His fingers trail from my hand to my wrist and up my arm as his face inches closer to mine.

My heart is thumping. Every bit of skin that his fingers touch is set on fire, and I feel like my body is about to burst. I lick my lips as his eyes flick down to watch the movement. He moves his hand a bit further up toward my elbow and moves his head ever so slightly closer to mine.

We're going to kiss. I know we are. I want to, and I know that he wants to. I don't know if I've ever wanted anything more in my entire life. Our faces are inches apart and I can feel his hot breath washing over my cheek as he leans in.

"Yoo-hoo!" A voice calls out. The two of us fall backward and I look over to see Cecilia rounding the corner and heading toward us. "Wow! The place looks great!"

I stand up and brush my clothes off, only to cover them with more dirt from my hands. Aiden jumps up and clears his throat before grabbing a nearby shovel and stabbing it into another garden plot. I force a smile at Cecilia while trying to control the violent beating of my heart.

She walks up with a huge smile on her face and talks incessantly, waving at the garden and saying things I can't quite understand yet. It takes a few moments for my brain to catch up as I force a smile and nod at Cecilia.

"Yeah, definitely," I say, hoping it makes sense with whatever she was talking about. She seems to accept my response and turns toward Aiden.

"I thought you were opposed to all this?" she says. Her voice sounds too loud, too piercing.

Aiden just grunts in response and I widen my eyes at Cecilia who shrugs in response. "*What!*" she mouths at me and I shake my head. I nod to a stack of plants.

"Can you bring me those, Cecilia? We can finish this plot." Aiden glances over at me and our eyes linger on each other. His eyes flick down to my lips and I can't resist trailing my own gaze down the length of his body. I stare just a second too long at his crotch, imagining the cock that I saw yesterday.

Cecilia appears beside me and I snap my head toward her, forcing a smile. We work together, planting the plants as she talks away about everything and nothing. After a few minutes, Aiden picks up his tools and nods.

"I've got to go. Good luck," he grunts. I open my mouth to speak but he's already walking away. It's not until the truck rumbles down the street that Cecilia looks at me and shakes her head.

"He's a bit of a brute, isn't he?" she says. My gaze snaps back to her and I frown.

"Just because he's quiet doesn't mean he's a brute!" I say. My words are more forceful than I intended, and Cecilia looks taken aback. Her eyebrows shoot up toward her hairline and she nods slowly.

"I was only saying... With his display at the town hall meeting and all, it seems a bit strange that he'd be here helping this morning." She cocks her head to the side and looks at me curiously. "Maybe he likes you."

I shake my head and snort. "Don't be ridiculous," I say, avoiding eye contact with her. I pat at the dark earth around a young plant and feel her stare on my face. My cheeks redden and I keep my gaze steady on the plants in the garden.

"Mmhmm," she says. I finally look at her and see the incredulous look painted on her face.

"What!" I protest. She laughs and shakes her head.

"Be careful, Madeline. Remember that you and he are on opposite sides of a very expensive coin here."

"There's nothing to be careful about, Cecilia," I say, standing up and grabbing a shovel. "Because nothing is going on."

"Right," she says. "You know, I was young too, once." She's staring at me, and I can almost feel the grin on her face even though I'm not looking at her. How much did she see, I wonder? She walked up as Aiden was touching my arm. Our faces must have been inches apart.

I shake my head. She didn't see anything, because there was nothing to see. She's still staring at me, so I ignore her and turn to another plot as Margaret McCoy appears and waves. "I brought friends!" she says, motioning to the other towns-people. "We should make great progress today!"

I force a smile and try to push Aiden Clark to the far, far back of my mind.

14

AIDEN

I ACCELERATE down the road a bit faster than I should. I don't know what just happened. Why was I there? I shouldn't have been there. My father's old truck revs down the main road until I turn off toward my cabin. As soon as I'm off the main road, I breathe a sigh of relief and feel my whole body relax.

Going into town was a mistake. Seeing Madeline was a mistake. Helping with the garden was a mistake. I should be opposing all their projects with everything I can, not *helping* them! I park the truck in front of the cabin and slide out, slamming the door behind me. I set off toward the forest without looking back at the pickup.

One step after another, I make my way through the forest, up the winding path toward the top of the mountain. The endlessness of the forests calms me down, and I take a deep, cleansing breath. I brush my fingers along the trees as I walk by and recite their names in my head, just as my father taught us.

Balsam fir, red maple, birch, spruce, aspen, eastern hemlock.

It's like a poem, running continuously through my mind as I put one foot in front of the other. I put more distance between me and Lang Creek, more distance between me and Maddy Croft. The narrow dirt path switches back to climb further up the mountain. Before I know it, I'm at the lookout where I stood with Maddy less than a day ago.

I climb up the boulder and look over the wide expanse of the countryside. The sun is still burning off the morning mist and I take another deep breath.

The mountains have always been a calming place for me. I've always felt at home here. But now, as I stand on this rock and stare out in the distance, all I can think about is Maddy's soft exhale when she saw it for the first time. My fingers tingle at the thought of her hand slipping into mine. I can still see the brightness in her eyes as she gazed upon the Adirondacks from up here for the first time in her life.

It doesn't feel calming to me now. It feels empty and meaningless. I turn my back on the awe-inspiring landscape and head up higher toward the tree-line. As I get higher, the trees start to thin until there are only a handful of pine trees dotting the mountainside. The air is thinner already, and I feel that familiar tightening in my chest when I get nearer to a summit.

My breath is more labored but I push on, putting one foot in front of another until all that's left are a few shrubs and loose rocks. The scree rock slides under my feet and it feels like I'm constantly taking two steps forward and one step back. I zig-zag up the side of the mountain, keeping my head down and focusing on my where my next step will go. Almost all of a sudden, I'm at the top.

I look out across the countryside, spinning in a full circle as I take in the endless peaks that surround me. They feel like *my* mountains. They feel like *my* territory, *my* home. I can see Lang Creek spreading out at the base of the mountain, chimneys letting out thin tendrils of smoke. My eyes travel up the mountainside toward the patch of mountain that I know has been bought by Maddy's company.

Soon, those trees will be razed and all that will be left is a huge lump of a building on this mountain. I sit down on the summit and let my eyes wander from the peaks to the town to the site of the future hotel. A cold breeze lifts the edges of my jacket and I feel it pierce through my bones.

Suddenly, my chest feels tight and my eyes are prickling. I can feel my father all around me. I can almost see him in front of me, teaching me about the trees and the plants, guiding me to listen to the calls of the birds and even showing me the insects that make the whole forest regenerate. *Everyone plays a part*, he used to tell me.

I try to look toward Lang Creek but my eyes blur. If he were here, he wouldn't be chasing after some woman. He wouldn't be helping the corporation that's trying to destroy these forests that our family has called home for generations.

He wouldn't be standing up in front of the town to oppose the new hotel, only to let his cock guide him back to the woman who represents all that destruction. He wouldn't be living alone in a cabin, going to work for the family that stole everything from ours. He wouldn't have to put on coveralls that say,

'McCoy Trucking' and be reminded of their betrayal every day of the week.

Tears start streaming down my cheeks, and the cold breeze feels like it's freezing them against my skin. Every tear that falls feels like an icicle on my face, reminding me of my weakness and of my failure to live up to my father's standards.

He would have wanted more. He would have expected me to fight this with everything I had, and to guide the townspeople to follow me. He would have expected me to be a leader.

My tears keep falling as I look toward the town again. It feels like weakness, but I still want to know her. I still wish she was here, looking down at the town with me. I still want to show her what these mountains mean to me, to everyone that lives here.

I don't know what to think. I know I should be fighting this, but Maddy makes me feel more alive than I've felt since I was a teenager. I know I should want her to leave, but all I want is for her to stay as long as possible.

I stand up and spread my arms, leaning my head back and screaming as loud as I can. It rips through my chest and burns my throat as it passes through me, taking all my frustration and my confusion and my pain and sending it into the void.

The echo of my scream taunts me, bouncing off the mountains until it finally fades into silence. I brush my cheeks and shuffle my feet to warm them up again before turning back down toward the path.

I'm still confused. Still conflicted. Still unbearably attracted to Madeline Croft. The wind picks up again and I know I

need to put all that aside. These mountains are more important than me, more important than her, more important than
any of us. Whatever it is that Maddy has woken up inside me
needs to go back to sleep.

15

MADELINE

"THAT SOUNDS GREAT, MOM," I say, staring at the ceiling as I cradle my cell phone on my shoulder. "I wish I could have come."

"Your father is looking better already. Bianca has had the most wonderful time here! The weather is fantastic."

"That's great," I repeat, tracing the line where the wall meets the ceiling with my eyes. I know my mother is calling me to make me feel guilty for not going to Miami with them, but I refuse to give in. "Can I talk to Dad?"

"Sure," she says. "He's right here."

"Hi, Mads," my father's deep voice comes on over the phone. I smile and sit up.

"Hey, Dad. How are you feeling?"

"Oh, you know," he says vaguely. "Getting old. How's work?"

I shake my head and grin. He always brings things back to work. "It's okay. We're having a hard time getting the townspeople on board with the project."

"Do you believe in it?"

His question surprises me, and I stand up before answering. I run my fingers through my hair and pace back and forth in my hotel room. I take a deep breath.

"Yeah, I do," I say. "It's a beautiful part of the world, and it'll bring a lot of tourism and jobs to the area. It'll be a huge injection of money into the town."

My father chuckles. "Mads," he starts. "I've run companies my whole life. You don't have to feed me that bullshit. Do you believe in the project?"

I take a deep breath. I wish I was with him right now, resting my head on his shoulder. He's always been there to guide me whenever I needed it.

"I'm not sure," I finally admit. "I thought I was. I mean, it's the biggest project that I've ever worked on. I'm the lead environmental engineer and it's a clear step forward in my career. But the other day, one of the guys in town showed me the forest that we'll be building in and –" I stop talking, not sure what I want to tell my dad. Should I tell him about Aiden? What is there to tell? I take a deep breath. "I don't know, Dad, it's so beautiful out here. It seems like a shame to build a big old hotel in the middle of it."

My father makes a noise and I can almost picture him nodding slowly. He strokes his chin when he's mulling over a problem, and I imagine that's what he's doing right now.

"There's one thing I've learned in all my years, Madeline," he says. "You have to stay true to yourself." My chest tightens and I'm not sure how to respond. I'm not even really sure what he's trying to tell me. I hear him take a deep wheezing breath and he continues.

"I've always been proud of you, Mads. Going off on your own and pursuing the environmental degree – I've always respected that in you. You and I are very similar."

My heart squeezes some more, and the corners of my eyes start to prickle with tears. I nod and try to swallow. "Thanks, Dad," I croak.

"I mean it. Obviously, I would have liked you to come work for me and take over the company, but you need to find your own way. If this project isn't what you thought it was, then you need to be true to yourself."

I nod and keep pacing back and forth. "I don't know, Dad. It's hard to tell."

"Give it a bit more time. You've just mobilized to site a few days ago, and construction hasn't truly started. Keep talking to the townspeople and keep following your instincts. You won't be far off."

"Thanks, Dad," I reply. Before he can answer, I hear him cough violently on the other end of the line. I frown, holding the phone to my ear as I wait for him to quiet down. It seems to take forever for his breathing to return to normal. I hear my mother fussing in the background and my dad finally speaks again.

"I better go now, Mads. Take care."

"Love you," I say. My chest feels like it's squeezing harder than ever before.

"Love you too, kiddo." We hang up the phone and I hold it to my heart, letting the tears fall down my cheeks. I sit on the edge of my bed and mull over his words.

I've always thought of my father as the career man, the company man, the CEO. He's always put work first, even when I wished he would pay more attention to me and my sister. But now, he's telling me to follow my heart. He's telling me to listen to my instincts and to do what I think is best.

He's telling me he respects me, and that he's proud of me.

The tears are falling fast now and my cheeks are completely wet. I thought my father was disappointed in me and that he thought my career was going nowhere. To hear him say those words makes me feel like I'm floating, but knowing that he's sick makes the whole conversation bittersweet.

I take a deep breath and flop backward on the bed. Aiden Clarke's face appears in my mind. I think of the way he looks at the forest, the way he reveres the mountains. He worships these lands, and he thinks the hotel is a bad idea.

Maybe that's all the convincing I need? Maybe I should just listen to him and let myself be convinced that this hotel is not the right thing to do. But where would that leave me? I'd have to leave my job and everything I've worked for. I've always thought environmental engineering was the way forward for me, but for the first time I'm starting to think that might not be true.

As these thoughts are swirling in my head, my computer dings with a new email. I stand up and frown as I look at the screen.

My applications to the federal and state governments have been approved. The Department of Environmental Conservation has given the green light for the construction of the project. Within seconds, another email from Barry comes through. He congratulates me and sets the date for project mobilization in three weeks. All the planning and preparation that our team has been doing is now set in motion.

The construction of the hotel at Lang Creek is going full-steam ahead.

16

——————

AIDEN

THE DAYS MELD together and I fall back into my regular routine. I stay on the mountain except when I need to go to work. I drive to the maintenance yard, avoiding Lang Creek and its residents, avoiding the hotel, avoiding Maddy. No one bothers me up here. I'm free to work on the cabin, to work on my cars, my garden, whatever I want.

I don't have to think about anything except what I'll be doing today.

Once in a while, when dusk starts to settle and the stars start to come out, my mind drifts to that morning in the community garden. I think of how smooth Maddy's skin was, and how bright her eyes were when I touched her arm. I think of the way my whole body was set on fire and how I felt alive for the first time in years.

It's been almost two weeks since that morning, or maybe three, I've lost count. I think it's Friday today. I'm just waking up to see the dew on the grass outside and the sunlight filtering through the trees. I open the front door to the cabin and stretch my arms overhead before frowning as I hear the rumble of a vehicle coming up the road.

The last few times someone's been up here, it's always been about that damn hotel and it's always brought bad news. I pull on a sweater and wait for the car to come into view. I listen hard, trying to recognize the engine. It doesn't sound like my brother's truck, or any truck for that matter. It's a smaller car.

When it finally rounds the bend my brows knit together and I frown. This is worse than the Sheriff, it's worse than Madeline, it's worse than anyone else.

It's Mara McCoy.

She looks at me through the windshield as she parks the car, and I feel ice flow through my veins as I look at the face that caused me so much pain. She turns off the engine and gets out, closing the door gently and staring at me without saying a word.

We stand there, facing off, for what feels like an eternity. Finally, she takes a step toward me and I speak.

"What do you want?" I bark. She stops and lifts her chin up at me with the familiar defiance that I used to love.

"I came to see you," she says. Her voice sounds just like it did ten years ago. My chest feels like it's collapsing and the skin on my face tightens against my bones.

"What do you want," I repeat. She stares at me for a moment and waves a hand in front of her face. I see the glint of a ring on her finger.

"I'm spending a few weeks in town. I thought I should tell you," she says. Her voice is terse, but I don't care. She takes another step toward me before speaking again. "I'm getting married."

I've thought about this moment for ten years. I thought it would hurt. I thought I'd be enraged, or angry. I thought I would care.

But when I look at her, all I see is the past. All I see is the pain that she caused my family and the lack of remorse that somehow stung even more.

"Congratulations," I growl.

"Aiden..." she says slowly. "The way things ended between us..."

"What," I interrupt. "Did you come here to apologize? After everything? After ten years? You're getting married and now you want a clear conscience, is that it?" I bark. "You killed my father, and then your family stole his business from us!"

She stares at me, her eyes hardening before she turns around and opens the door to her car.

"You're a fucking asshole, you know that? I'm glad you're up here all alone. No woman should ever have to put up with you."

The venom in her voice only fuels my anger. "You destroyed my family and then stole everything my father worked for," I spit. "Get the fuck out of here."

She opens her mouth to protest and I think I see a tear in her eye, but she turns her head and gets into her car. I don't wait for her to drive away. I just turn around and head off toward the mountainside. I stomp my feet along the path and let the anger course through my veins.

The gall of her! The fucking nerve, to come up here and announce her marriage! Like I would fucking care! My whole body feels heavier and I push the memories of my father's accident further down. I can't think of it, not now. I can't deal with that pain.

I let the searing anger wash over me like a tidal wave until I'm surrounded by trees. Even the birds have gone quiet, and it's just me and my anger, stomping through the woods.

She's the one who wanted to go to the river that day. She's the one who wanted to walk on the edge, even when the river was swollen with spring snowmelt. She's the one who stumbled, and she's the one who my father tried to save.

His death ripped my heart out of my chest. I've never felt pain like that before. At least, not until her family betrayed mine and stole everything my father had worked for.

She never loved me. She never wanted to be with me. She just wanted what I had. And now she's found some other fool to suck completely dry.

I can hardly see. Branches scratch my face as I crash through the forest. Twigs break underfoot as I make my way deeper and deeper into the woods. Finally, I lean against a tree and feel my chest heave up and down as I try to slow my racing heart.

This is why I don't go into town. This is why I avoid the McCoys. It's too painful. The past is too hard to face. It seems like everyone has moved on – except for me.

I stand up taller and take a deep breath, looking around to get my bearings. I didn't even follow a path, I just walked straight into the forest and away from *her*. I spin around and look up at the sun to orient myself when I hear a noise.

It sounds almost like a woman's voice. It's a yell, far in the distance, muffled by the undergrowth and the trees. I frown and for the second time today, listen hard to the distant sound.

I take a few gentle steps toward the sound and hear it more clearly. It's definitely a woman's voice. She's yelling. I walk gently, listening intently and heading in her direction.

All thoughts of Mara McCoy evaporate. All thoughts of my father, of the past, of the pain in my heart disappear as I head toward the sound. As I get closer, alarm bells start ringing inside me. I know that voice. I've only heard it a couple times, but it's been burned in my mind since the town hall meeting two weeks ago.

My footsteps get faster. I'm sure now, it's her. It's Maddy, and she's in trouble.

17

———

MADELINE

Rule number one of hiking is never go out on your own without telling anyone. I know that, and I still did it. When we got let off work early for the weekend, I thought it would be the perfect day to go explore the edges of the hotel's property.

I stare at the huge tree that's pinning me down and I try to wriggle free. Pain shoots up through my leg and I wince. Maybe it wasn't such a good idea after all.

"Help!" I yell out again, knowing that there's no one for miles. I reach down and try to get my hand into my pocket. My fingertips just brush the edge of my phone and I strain to get a grip on it. I yell out again, and stretch my hand a bit further into my pocket. The tree is pinning me down, putting intense pressure on my legs. I try to wiggle my toes and I know I don't have much time. It doesn't feel like anything is broken, but soon my circulation will be cut off and then I'll be in real trouble.

My fingers slip on the edge of my phone and I claw at it in my pocket. I shift a fraction of an inch and get a grip on the edge of it, finally sliding it out.

"Yes!" I exclaim under my breath, bringing the phone up to my face. The screen is smashed, but I can still turn it on. I glance up at the top corner and my heart drops when I see the two little words I was dreading: *No Service*.

"Fuck."

I crane my neck and look around again, yelling out. I frown as I hear something in the distance. It sounds like an animal moving around – a large animal. My heart starts thumping in my chest and I squint, trying to see through the thick under-growth in the direction of the sound.

It's coming straight for me.

My heart is thumping in my chest and I try to wriggle myself free. "Come on, come on, fuck!" I yell, moving my legs back and forth and trying to push the log off me.

It's no use. Ever since I slipped down the slope and lodged myself under this tree, I've known I was in trouble. My legs are pinned, and the wet leaves underneath me aren't providing anything to grip on.

I'm stuck.

The noise is getting closer. It sounds like a huge animal crashing through the forest, barreling straight toward me.

A moose? Or worse – a bear?

I look in that direction again and feel the tears start gathering in the corners of my eyes. Whatever animal it is, it's headed directly at me. I close my eyes and lean back, letting the tears fall down my face as I start to accept my fate.

I hope they find me, even if I'm half-eaten by this bear. Then they can send my body back to my parents and at least they'll know what happened to me. At least I won't have to watch my father deteriorate any more.

All these thoughts of doom and gloom fill my head until the animal crashing through the underbrush starts yelling my name. I lift my head up in shock, turning toward the noise.

"Maddy?" The voice calls out. "Maddy where are you?"

"Here!" I scream, louder than before. My throat feels raw but I scream louder as hope fills me up like a balloon. "I'm here!"

He comes into view like my knight in shining armor, except he's wearing a wooly plaid shirt. My heart jumps in my chest when I see Aiden rushing toward me, his face drawn with worry.

"Watch out!" I say, pointing to the spot where I slid. He jumps over it and lowers himself slowly down toward me.

"Are you hurt?" he says. His eyebrows are pulled together and his voice is deep and gravelly.

"I'm not sure," I say. "My leg hurts but I don't know how bad it is."

Aiden glances at the tree and at my leg underneath. He spends a minute looking all around and then glances back at my face.

"I don't see any blood," he says. "Can you move your feet?" I nod, and he nods back. "I'm going to lift this tree. Do you think you can pull yourself out while I lift it?"

"I'll try," I say.

It's all the go-ahead he needs. I watch as he wraps his muscular arms around the huge tree trunk and lifts it up two or three inches. I brace myself against the log and slide out from under it, wincing as pain shoots through my leg. I shuffle upwards until I'm clear of the tree and he drops it back down again, crawling toward me.

"What happened? What are you doing here on your own?"

Before I know it, I'm sobbing like a child. He wraps his arms around me and pulls me in close so that my face is buried in his chest. All I do is sob and breathe in his fresh piney musk. He squeezes me close and then lets go, glancing down at my leg.

"Can you walk?"

I shrug, and Aiden puts his arm under my back. He pulls me back up to the path where I slipped and tries to put me upright. The instant I put weight on my right leg, pain shoots through my ankle. I groan and my eyes water. Aiden pulls me closer and puts his arm around me.

"Come on," he says. In one smooth motion, he swings me up so that I'm cradled in his arms. "Watch the branches. I'll take you back to the cabin."

I nestle my head in his chest and try to hide the tears in my eyes. My heart is still thumping and my head is spinning. I can hardly believe what's happened. I went from going for a quiet walk to thinking I would be eaten by a bear, only to be rescued by the man I've been fantasizing about for the past two weeks.

The pain in my leg fades as I wrap my arms around his neck and let myself melt into him. Even though I know I was stupid to head out on my own, and I've been incredibly lucky for him to find me, it almost feels like fate. It feels like we were meant to find each other and we're supposed to be together.

He squeezes me a bit closer and looks down at me for a moment. Our eyes meet and I see a deep pain in his eyes.

"Don't do that again," he growls. "Don't go off on your own."

"I won't," I whisper. "I promise."

He holds me closer and I let the tears fall from my eyes into his chest as he carries me all the way back to his cabin.

18

———

AIDEN

SHE FEELS SO small in my arms. I try to shield her from the low-hanging branches that might scratch her while I make my way back to the nearest path. I know these woods like the back of my hand, but I still wish I could get back quicker.

I don't know why she was there, or why she was alone, or how long she was pinned under that tree, but none of that matters now. All I care about is getting her back to safety and making sure she's alright. As much as I hate to admit it, I'm starting to be glad that Mara showed up at my place. If it wasn't for her, I never would have found Maddy.

I look down and see her crying softly. My chest squeezes for the thousandth time today, but this time it's not anger, or pain. I just want to protect her. I glance at her leg and hope it's not broken.

Finally, we get to the main path and I know we're less than ten minutes away from my cabin.

"I'm going to drive you to the hospital. You're going to need an x-ray," I say. She nods but says nothing. We go the rest of the way in silence. By the time we make it to my truck, the sweat is dripping down between my shoulder blades and my arms and legs are screaming from the effort.

I place her down gently and open the door of the truck. Before she gets in, she puts a hand on my chest and looks up at my face.

"Aiden," she says softly. I shake my head.

"It's okay."

"Thank you," she says. She lifts her other hand to my chest and it crawls up toward my neck. I catch it with my palm and bring her fingers up to my lips. I kiss them softly, staring deep into her eyes. She straightens her fingers and runs them along my jaw until they're wrapped around the base of my neck.

The instant our lips touch, it feels like this is where I was meant to be. Our bodies melt together and I wrap my arms around her. She curls her fingers into my hair and presses herself into me as our lips crush together and I finally get to taste her.

A soft moan slips out of her lips and I kiss her harder, not wanting this moment to end. I wrap my arm around the small of her back and bring her just a bit closer to me until her body stiffens and I remember that she's in pain.

"Sorry," I breathe, pulling away from her.

She shakes her head. "It's fine." Her eyes linger on mine for a moment until I nod to the truck.

"We'd better get you checked out."

She gets into the truck and I jog over to the driver's side. Once the engine turns over, she slips her hand over my leg and my cock twitches toward her. I glance over at her and she smiles shyly.

"Thank you," she says again. "I thought I was going to die out there."

"You could have," I growl. "What were you doing out there?"

She winces and I immediately regret my words. I've been on my own too long, I don't know how to act around women anymore. If I'm honest, I don't know how to act around people anymore.

"I just needed some air. Work has gotten intense, and I'm just..." She pauses. "I'm just not sure about it all anymore."

I nod but say nothing. I'm not sure what she means, but I just stare straight ahead and try to focus on the road. Her hand is still on my thigh, burning through my pants and breathing life into my whole body. I can't focus on anything except her taste on my lips, her hand on my thigh, and trying my best to not crash this truck.

We drive in silence toward the nearest hospital. It's in the next town over, and I'm silently thankful for the extra time together.

The silence doesn't feel forced or awkward, it just feels natural. It feels like we've known each other forever, and we're just comfortable in each other's company. I don't remember the last time I felt like that with another person, let alone a woman.

I glance over at her as she stares out the window and my heart squeezes again. I wish she wasn't working for that fucking hotel construction company. I wish we'd met under different circumstances.

The big 'H' in front of the hospital comes into view and I pull up in front of the emergency doors. A nurse comes out to talk to us and brings out a wheelchair. She points me over to the parking lot and I watch her wheel Maddy inside the hospital.

Even being away from her for five minutes feels wrong. I just want to be near her – from now until I know for sure she'll be okay.

She never should have been out there on her own. If I hadn't run off in a blind rage through the woods, I never would have found her. She was on the border of my property and the hotel's. No one ever goes there. I shake my head and try not to think about what would have happened if I hadn't found her.

I park the car and take a deep breath. Maybe Mara coming to see me was a blessing in disguise. If she hadn't come, I wouldn't have gone out in the woods. I wouldn't have found Maddy, and I wouldn't have brought her back. I wouldn't have kissed her and held her in my arms. I wouldn't be here with her now.

I mull over these thoughts as I lock the truck and head toward the bright hospital doors. They slide open as I walk through, and from the waiting area I see Maddy turn her head toward me. Her face lights up and I feel a smile forming on my lips.

"I thought you'd left," she says in a low voice when I slide my hand onto her shoulder.

"I'm not going anywhere," I reply. She intertwines her fingers into mine and gives them a light squeeze. My heart thumps in

my chest and I sit down beside her, ready to wait as long as I
need to until she's patched up and released from the hospital.
I'm definitely not going anywhere.

19

—————

MADELINE

"YOU DIDN'T HAVE to stay. It took so long!" I say, silently grateful that Aiden is still beside me. He wheels me out of the hospital in the wheelchair and grunts in response. I feel a bit silly being wheeled out, but apparently, it's hospital policy. My ankle is only lightly sprained, and the doctor said that once the swelling goes down it should be better within a few days. I'm so lucky, I can't even wrap my head around it.

Aiden loads the crutches into the back of the truck and jogs over to the passenger side door. He helps me up out of the wheelchair and I climb into the seat, smiling at him in thanks. I watch him walk around the front of the pickup and open the driver's side door.

The past couple hours have flown by. Thankfully, the hospital wasn't busy and I didn't have to wait too long, but it was still just over two hours, most of which we spent in silence.

As usual with Aiden, though, it was a comfortable silence. I turn to look at him as he drives out of the hospital, and my heart squeezes at the thought of going back to the McCoy's hotel. I don't want to leave him. We drive in silence for a few miles until I clear my throat.

"Aiden..."

"You want to come back to my place for a drink?" he interrupts. He keeps his eyes straight ahead on the road and my heart jumps in my chest. A lump forms in my throat and I nod my head up and down.

"Sure," I finally say in a hoarse whisper. I can feel a spark igniting between my legs as I think of going back to Aiden's cabin with him, alone in the woods with nothing but trees and mountains to surround us. I slide my hand over his thigh and he slides his fingers into it, curling them so that his palm covers my whole hand. I close my eyes, feeling safer and warmer than I've felt in weeks.

"Why were you up there alone?" he asks all of a sudden. I open my eyes again and glance over at him. My cheeks start to blush at the harshness of his voice.

"I know it was stupid," I start.

"You're fucking right it was," he says, turning his head to stare at me. His eyes are blazing and I see something in them. Is it concern? Does he care that much? "You could have died."

I try to swallow and I nod. "I know. I went up there after work. We'd just had a meeting about clearing the land to the north of the hotel site for a sports complex and the thought of it..." my voice trails off. I stare out the window at the passing scenery. The old forest is dense and dark as we drive back to his place in the dusk. "I wanted to see what we'd be building on." The last word comes out as a whisper and Aiden's hand tenses over mine. The veins in his neck bulge and he keeps his head staring forward. I can see his free hand gripping the steering wheel until his knuckles are white.

"Thank you for saving me," I say. "I know I shouldn't have been up there on my own. I owe you my life."

Aiden grunts in response and turns up the worn gravel path up toward his cabin. He parks the truck outside the cabin and jumps down, jogging around to help me out of the car.

"You want to use the crutches?" he asks. "You can lean on me. There won't be much room for them in there," he says, nodding to the small cabin.

"I'll be fine," I say, wrapping my arm around his waist. We hop toward his front door and he pushes it open. He guides me to a worn sofa and turns to the wood-burning stove in the middle of the room, lighting a fire in a few seconds. He disappears behind me and reappears with two cold beers in his hand. I take one and clink it gently against his before taking a long drink.

I sigh in satisfaction as the cold liquid travels down my throat.

"Thanks," I say, opening my eyes to see him staring at me.

"You're beautiful," he growls. My heart starts thumping in my chest. My tongue darts out to lick my lips and my whole body feels like it's electric. His eyes travel down from my face along my body. Everywhere his gaze touches feels like it's set on fire. He trails his eyes back up toward my face and runs his fingertips along my arm. I close my eyes and a moan escapes my lips as a shiver passes through my body.

His hand brushes across my shoulder and he wraps his fingers around the base of my neck. I don't have to open my eyes to know his face is inches from mine. I part my lips and wait for the taste of his kiss.

It's better than the first time. I wrap my arms around his neck and tangle my fingers into his hair as our lips crush together. He presses his body against mine and brings his other hand to my waist, pulling me closer to him. I lean back, falling on to the couch until his body is completely covering mine. He's holding himself up on his elbows but I pull his face toward mine, loving the weight of his body on top of me.

His erection is pressing into my stomach and I grind my hips up toward it. I can feel the heat of it through my clothes, and all I want to do is feel him thrust it inside me. I rock my hips back and forth until he moans as he kisses me, pressing himself down onto me.

He moves his mouth to kiss my ear, my neck. He pulls my shirt down to kiss my collarbone. I shiver as he kisses all along my collarbone toward my shoulder, and then takes his tongue and licks all the way back toward my chest. He moves his lips between my breasts and runs his fingers over to squeeze the soft flesh of my breasts.

My body is on fire. It's screaming for him, screaming for his touch, his kiss, his cock. I grind myself into him and gasp as his lips move back up toward mine. He kisses me with a hunger I've never felt before. It's like he wants to taste every part of me, to devour me with every kiss.

I run my hands along his shoulders and finally feel the muscles that I've been staring at every time I see him. I dig my fingertips into his neck and bring his face to mine again, locking our lips together and kissing him harder. He groans and presses himself on top of me, finally lifting his head up and running his hand along my cheek.

"I've wanted to do this since the first time I saw you at that meeting," he growls. His words send a thrill straight to my core, and the heat in my stomach blossoms. I run my fingers across his temple and back into his hair, watching him groan in satisfaction as he closes his eyes.

"You're so fucking sexy," I whisper. He opens his eyes again and I see something else in them, something wilder than I've seen before. There's a depth to his desire that makes my whole body feel like it's burning. It's animalistic, almost savage. His eyes stare into mine and for a moment, we're completely frozen.

I feel his growl more than I hear it. It rumbles through his chest and into my body as his fingers curl on my breast. He pushes his hips down onto me and I feel his hard cock pressing into me again. I moan as he does it, and he growls again before grabbing my shirt and yanking it down.

The fabric rips and I gasp. My shirt hangs open to reveal my black bra and the white skin of my stomach. He growls again, dropping his head to kiss the skin between my breasts. I run my fingers through his hair and feel him groan again.

The space between my legs is burning with desire. His hands grip my waist as he runs his tongue down the center of my stomach, igniting a fire in my veins.

"Aiden," I breathe, unable to think of anything else to say. He glances up at me, meeting my eye for just an instant before dipping his head back down toward the waistband of my pants.

20

AIDEN

When she says my name, it makes my whole body buzz. I never knew I liked my own name so much until I heard it from her lips, in that breathy whisper that's loaded with pure desire.

I run my fingers back up her sides and reach behind to unclasp her bra. She sits up and I slide it off her body. I groan as I see her breasts for the first time. The ripped fabric of her ruined shirt falls off her body and puddles on the floor. I catch her nipple between my lips, swirling my tongue around it as my free hand grabs her other breast. I groan as she bucks her hips toward me, moaning every time I touch her.

My cock is straining against my pants. I want nothing more than to plunge it deep inside her and feel her walls contract around me as I pump my seed deep into her. I want nothing more than to take her body and claim her right now. She moans again and my whole body shivers in response.

I move my lips to her other breast, kissing it before taking her nipple gently between my teeth. She gasps as I run my tongue around her areola, and then trail kisses between her breasts and back down her stomach. My hands linger over her breasts before running down her sides toward the waistband of her pants. I hook my fingers into her pants and let my tongue run over and back across her stomach. She whimpers, writhing toward me as I taste her skin.

I sit up, gazing at her body as she lies back on the couch. She bites her lip and my cock twitches again, and I watch as her fingers trail down her chest. She squeezes her own breasts and I groan, feeling the heat in my body increase by a few degrees as I watch her touch herself. Her hands move from her breasts, following the path of my mouth just moments before toward her stomach.

She unbuttons her pants and slowly slides the zipper down. My heart is thumping in my chest and the heat of desire courses through my veins. I rip my shirt off over my head and feel her hands on my stomach. I lean forward, letting her explore my chest and stomach with her hands for a few moments. I close my eyes and groan at her touch, loving the way her fingers run across every ridge of my muscles, every bone, every inch of my skin.

She runs her fingers all the way up to my shoulders and down my arms, and then back across to my chest and down my stomach. She dips her fingertips into the waistband of my pants and I feel myself losing control. Her fingers just brush the base of my cock and a growl rises in my chest. My cock is so hard it hurts, straining against my pants until I feel like I'm going to explode before she even touches it.

I'm straddling her on the couch, with both her legs between mine. I shift my weight and see her wince.

"Fuck, sorry Maddy," I say, remembering her sprained ankle.

"Who cares," she breathes. "Take off your fucking pants."

I grin and nod, standing up to let my pants fall down. I pull down my jocks and my cock springs free, the tip of it already wet with my precum. Maddy gasps, sitting up on her elbows before shimmying her pants down her legs. The instant I see that little patch of pubic hair above her slit, I lose all control.

I dive forward, lifting her legs up onto my shoulders and covering her slit with my mouth. I groan as the salty sweetness of her desire hits my tongue. I slide my tongue up and back until I hear her moan and her legs tense on my shoulders. I reach a hand up and press on her stomach, using my other hand to tease her opening. She whimpers again, and I lift my head up for an instant to watch her face.

Her hazel eyes are half-closed, and she runs her fingers through my hair. She shakes her head gently from side to side as she watches me, licking her lips and exhaling.

"Aiden," she breathes.

I don't wait for anything else. My lips find her bud and I let the heat of my breath tease her for an instant before running my tongue across it. She gasps as I kiss and lick and swirl my tongue over her bud, still circling her opening with my fingertips.

She's moaning and bucking her hips and gripping my hair and I don't know if I've ever been this turned on. She tastes so fucking good I can hardly believe it's possible. I take that bundle of nerves between my lips and finally plunge my fingers inside her as she lets out a long moan.

Feeling her walls grip my fingers almost makes me come. They slide inside her smoothly and her body contracts around them. She's gushing wetness as I reach to find that little rough patch of skin inside her. Her body contracts again. It feels like I can feel every sensation with her. When my lips touch her bud and when my fingers push inside her, her body lifts up toward me. She moans in a way that sets my blood on fire. Every noise, every move, every time she wraps her fingers into my hair and pushes my face down onto her pussy makes my cock harder than before.

I move my tongue and fingers and lips and hands back and forth until her back arches and her moan becomes a scream. Her fingers curl into my hair and the wetness gushes out of her, covering my fingers with her pleasure. I keep my lips on her bud and my fingers inside her until she moves me back, trembling and panting in front of me.

Her eyes are glazed over with pleasure. Her lips are wet and her chest is heaving up and down. I slide my fingers out of her and place a gentle kiss on that little strip of pubic hair before crawling up on top of her. I lay my body on top of her, letting my cock rest between her legs to feel the wetness that's dripping out of her.

I kiss her gently, wanting her to taste herself and to know what I've just been enjoying. She shivers underneath me, wrapping her arms around my neck and moaning into my mouth. I pull away and stare into her eyes, chuckling softly.

"You liked that?" I whisper.

"I've never... That was..." she stares at me and shakes her head. "Aiden..."

I place my lips against hers and kiss her gently. It doesn't matter what part of her body that I kiss, everything tastes incredible. From her lips to the apex of her thighs to the skin on her stomach, it tastes like it was made for me.

She moans again and runs her fingers through my hair and down my back. Her body trembles one more time before she grinds her hips up toward me. I lift my head up and see a glimmer in her eye. I grin.

"You want more already?"

"I'm greedy," she breathes. "I always want more."

21

MADELINE

My orgasm is still coursing through my body, sending shocks of pleasure to every extremity. I can finally see straight again, and the feeling of Aiden's cock against my body is driving me wild.

I've never had anyone eat me out like that before. He seemed to enjoy it as much as I did, and the thought of him being turned on by giving me pleasure was enough to send me over the edge. Now he's lifting himself up and I run my fingers over his chest one more time. My fingers trail down toward his cock. He groans as I wrap my fingers around his girth, stroking the soft skin up and down as my other hand keeps tracing the outline of his abdominal muscles.

Aiden runs his fingers up my thigh and grabs the side of my ass. He pulls me toward him as I stroke his cock, his eyes closed and his groans rumbling through his chest.

He's like an animal, and it's turning me on more than ever before. His cock is pulsing between my fingers, and the veins are bulging under my hand. The tip of his cock looks red and enlarged. My mouth starts to water as I watch my hand moving up and down his thick shaft. He groans again, squeezing my ass and moving his hips back and forth in time with my hand.

"You have a condom?" I ask, praying he says yes. I don't know if I'd be able to stop now if he doesn't have one. The desire rushing through me is making my head spin.

Aiden nods once and gets up. Even with the fire roaring in the wood stove just beside us, it's colder now that he's gone. I sit up on my elbows and watch him disappear into the back room. I see a neatly made bed through the opening of the door before Aiden reappears with a silver package in his hand. His cock swings from side to side with every step, and I watch it, mesmerized. He stands in front of me and opens the package, sliding the condom over his cock in a smooth motion.

I spread my legs, wincing as an arrow of pain shoots up from my ankle. I ignore it, turning my focus to Aiden and that beautiful cock of his. He kneels on the couch between my legs and groans as I spread myself wide for him. He slides his index and middle finger into his mouth and drags them up my slit, from my opening up to my bud. My head falls back and I moan as a shiver of pleasure passes up through my stomach and dissipates into my body.

He groans as his fingers slide back down and into my opening. I clench my walls down around him, wishing it was his cock that was inside me.

Aiden grabs the base of his cock with one hand as he glides the fingers of his other hand in and out of me. He watches my face, his eyes half-closed as my body trembles. I want him. I reach my hands down and run my fingers along his hip, down to his thigh.

"Fuck me, Aiden," I breathe.

He grins. "Say it again," he says, pushing his fingers deeper inside me. I arch my back and whimper as I feel the tips of his fingers touch my most sensitive spot. Another wave of pleasure starts to build inside me and I open my eyes to watch him grabbing his cock, teasing me as he brings it closer to my center.

"Fuck me, Aiden," I say.

Aiden's eyes close and he breathes out, pushing his fingers inside me one more time. "Beg me," he growls. He opens his eyes and I see that same animalistic desire burning inside him. He fucks me with his fingers a little bit faster and I feel like I could come right now. I gasp as he curls his fingers up and sends another thrill through my body. "Beg me," he whispers again.

I'm so turned on right now I feel like I can't do anything except lie here in a puddle of my own desire. I'd beg him to do anything right now. I want his cock so bad my mouth is watering. I can't think of anything except the way his hand is gripping the base of his shaft and the way his fingers just aren't enough for me now.

"Please," I whisper. "Please fuck me." He growls again and I lick my lips. "I'm begging you," I say.

As soon as the words leave my lips, Aiden growls and shifts his hips. In one smooth motion, he takes his fingers out of me and plunges his cock inside me – from the tip all the way to the hilt. I gasp as my body stretches for him.

My head falls back and Aiden rocks his hips back and forth. I hear my own moans as if they were coming from someone else. I'm not in my own body anymore. I'm watching myself get fucked by the most beautiful man I've ever seen with the most beautiful cock I've ever experienced.

He thrusts himself inside me and every time his hips hit mine it sends a jolt of pleasure through me. I feel every inch of him. My hands claw at him, pulling him closer and deeper inside me as he drives his cock into me. His grunts send shivers through my body and I wrap my legs around his waist.

I think my ankle hurts, but I don't even know anymore. My whole body is alight with pleasure. My veins are full of fire. He braces his arm on the arm of the sofa above my head and drives himself into me a little bit deeper. I scream as the pressure in my stomach builds and builds until I know I'm going to come again.

When I came with his mouth on my bud, I thought I was done. I thought that was as good as it gets. But now, as Aiden's chest presses into mine, as his cock pushes deeper inside me and my walls grip down on his girth, I know I was wrong.

Our bodies move as one and I sink my fingers into his shoulders. I push my hips up toward him as he fucks me harder and harder, pushing himself deeper into me. The pressure in my stomach builds until all of a sudden, it explodes.

Aiden moans into my ear and I feel his breath on my shoulder as my body releases. My walls gush and his cock slides effortlessly in and out of me. My back arches and I wrap my arms and legs around him, moaning into his ear.

He bites his teeth down on my shoulder as he pushes himself deeper inside me. My body grips him tighter, contracting around his cock as my orgasm rocks through my entire body. Aiden moans again, fucking me deep and hard until I feel him release inside me.

He shivers and tenses. The muscles in his neck bulge and his eyes close as his cock throbs inside me. My own orgasm is starting to fade and I can enjoy the full sensation of his cock pumping inside me. I can feel everything. I gasp as he comes until he lowers himself down on top of me.

Our hearts are thumping against each other. My chest is heaving up and down with every breath, and my whole body feels electric. Both of us are covered in a thin sheen of sweat, but it doesn't matter. Nothing matters. The only thing that I care about right now is the pulsing of my body and the weight of his chest on top of me. I close my eyes and let out a breath.

"Whoa," I breathe. Aiden only grunts in response.

22

AIDEN

I DON'T KNOW how long it takes me to regain control over my body. I lift myself up, hoping I wasn't too heavy on top of her. I grab the condom and slide out of her, groaning as I stand up. Maddy smiles at me, wiping the hair off her forehead and sighing.

"That was nice," she says.

"It was better than nice," I reply with a grin. "I'm going to take a quick shower."

She nods and I walk toward the stack of clean laundry in the corner. I throw the condom out and grab a towel, heading out the door to the back of the cabin. The air is cold outside, and I rush toward the shower. I turn the water on as hot as it goes and stand under it, sighing in satisfaction. I close my eyes and stand under the hot stream, not moving at all for a few minutes.

My body is still buzzing from my orgasm. I can still feel little thrills passing from my cock, through my stomach and I groan as I enjoy every one of them.

I haven't had sex with a woman in a long time, but even so – I know that was different. We moved together like we'd known each other our whole lives.

I almost jump when I feel two hands circling around my waist. I turn around to see Maddy coming into the shower with me. I wrap my arms around her and tuck a strand of hair behind her ear.

"I've never showered outside before," she says with a smile.

"First time for everything," I answer. I dip my chin down and kiss those irresistible lips of hers, letting my hand drop to the small of her back to pull her closer to me. The blood is heading toward my cock again already. Just having her near me is enough to make me hard.

She turns toward the water and grabs the bar of soap on the shower ledge. She's leaning on her good leg, and I wonder how she got all the way to the shower. She must have hopped here from the front door.

She soaps up her hands and faces me, washing my chest in slow circles. I groan and close my eyes, enjoying the soft touch of her hands against my body. She turns me around, washing my back, trailing her hands down to my ass. She wraps her hands around me and slowly, gently, strokes my cock. The soap makes her hand glide smoothly over my cock and I groan as it starts to get hard again.

"What are you doing to me?" I growl. I turn back around toward her and take the soap from her hand. It's my turn to lather her up. I let my hands glide along her body, running my palms over her breasts and squeezing them gently before soaping up her stomach. I wrap my arms around her to wash her back, pushing her long hair out of the way. She runs her fingers along my spine as I wash her. My hands drop to her ass and I reach my fingers down to brush the lips between her legs.

Maddy moans, moving her hips toward me. I squeeze her bottom and brush my fingers along her slit again, trailing them back up along the crack of her ass. She whimpers again and a growl rumbles in my chest.

"You want more already?" I ask, pulling away from her. I rest my hands on her waist as she runs her fingers over my chest. The water is pouring down between us and the steam is billowing up. She drops her hand and grabs my cock, pulling it gently as it gets hard between her fingers.

I drop my hand down her stomach and run my fingers through that little strip of hair above her slit. She moans as my fingers slide between her legs, and I groan as I feel how wet she is already.

I'd fuck her right here, but I see her wince as she accidentally puts weight on her sprained ankle. Instead, I turn her toward the water and rinse all the soap off her body. I take her lips in mine and kiss her tenderly, wrapping my arms around her and enjoying the closeness of our bodies under the water.

I rinse myself and turn off the water. The chill in the air immediately invades the shower and I smile as I watch Maddy's nipples get hard right away. I run my thumbs over them and kiss her lips one more time. I grab the towel and wrap her in it, lifting her up and throwing her over my shoulder. She yelps and laughs.

"What are you doing!" she exclaims.

"You're injured," I answer, walking back toward the front door. My cock is hard and heavy between my legs already, and all I can think about is the wetness between hers. The cold air doesn't bother me, nor does the fact that I'm completely naked. I carry her inside, ignoring the wet footsteps I leave all over the floor. I take her all the way to the bedroom and lay her down. She giggles as she lies back, the towel falling open to reveal her perfect body.

She slides the towel out from under her and runs it over my body. I groan, loving the way she touches me. Finally, I can't take it anymore. I reach over to the bedside table and take another condom out of the old box I keep there. I rip it open and slide it on.

This time I'm not teasing her. I'm not waiting or asking her to beg me. I'm sliding my fingers along her jaw and kissing her deeply, and then sliding my cock inside her once again.

I push it all the way in and she moans again, her walls stretching and twitching against my girth. I leave it there without moving, choosing instead to kiss her once more. She wraps her arms and legs around me and we move slowly, kissing and touching each other. We take our time, exploring each other's bodies in a way that we rushed through before.

When she comes, I feel it all. I feel her walls contract and I feel her body tense and then relax. I watch as her eyes close and her lips fall open. I kiss her again because no matter how many times our lips touch, I still can't get enough of her taste.

When I come, it's not as intense as the last time, but it's somehow *more*. My orgasm builds slowly and releases through my entire body. I empty myself into her and groan as she wraps herself around me even more tightly.

We fall asleep with our arms and legs intertwined, with her head on my shoulder and my lips against her forehead. For the first time in years, I feel completely and utterly at home.

23

MADELINE

I WAKE up with Aiden's arms around me. My ankle is a bit sore, but I move it up and down and am relieved to find that I've got more range of motion than I did before.

Aiden is snoring lightly in my ear. I turn my head to look at him and smile. Last night was as amazing as it was unexpected. He rescued me from the forest and took me home, and I enjoyed every minute of it. I never would have thought that getting stuck under a tree would be the best thing to ever happen to me.

My thoughts drift to yesterday, to the moments before I slipped and fell to wedge myself under the tree. I was stomping along the hillside, questioning everything about my job.

I've always thought I was doing good work. *I am one of the good guys*, or at least that's what I always tell myself. I've always thought that men like my father, who just extract resources from the land without a thought about the environment were the bad guys.

This time, it's different. This time, when the approved application to the Department of Environmental Conservation came through my email, all I felt was dread. All I still feel is dread. I'm starting to wonder if I'm on the wrong side of this battle.

Even though my job is to make sure that my company complies with all the regulations, it's not enough. We're still clear-cutting large swaths of land to build a hotel that most people in the area don't want. I'm one of the people that's helping to do that. As much as I tell myself that I'm doing a good thing, that I'm protecting the environment from inevitable development – something inside me is starting to change.

I'm not doing a good thing. In fact, I'm enabling my company to do this work. I'm not protecting the environment from them. I'm helping them to destroy these forests. Sure, if I wasn't doing it, I'd be replaced in an instant with someone else who would. But my father's words have been ringing through my head for two weeks now.

Stay true to yourself.

He told me he was proud of me, for going off and getting my environmental engineering degree. For pursuing my 'passion', whatever that is. Is this my passion? Making half a small town hate me all the while making a big hotel chain a bunch of money?

This isn't what I thought it would be. Environmental engineering, construction, conservation – none of it is what I thought it would be. I've come to hate the word 'sustainability', because it's just one of those words that men in suits throw around that doesn't actually mean anything.

Aiden snorts beside me and rolls over, dragging his arm with him. I watch his chest rise and fall and feel my own heart squeeze.

I feel more at home here with him than I do in New York, going to my corporate job and telling myself that I'm doing something good.

Walking through the woods feels good. Learning about the plants and animals that live here feels good. Building a community garden and getting to know the people of Lang Creek feels good. Going to work and seeing the mobilization of excavators, dump trucks, chipper trucks, and huge loads of materials does *not* feel good.

The day after tomorrow is Monday, and I have to go back to work. The site offices are ready and most of the preliminary team is here, so the official start of construction is in less than 48 hours. That thought used to fill me with excitement. It's my first big job! It's the first job where I've been leading the environmental team. Now, the thought of starting construction only fills me with dread. Aiden snorts beside me again, as if he can feel the turmoil in my heart.

I can't take it anymore. I'm driving myself crazy, lying here thinking about these things. I slide out of bed and shiver as the cold morning air in the cabin hits my body. I grab the closest piece of clothing – one of Aiden's shirts, and I slip into it. It goes all the way down to my knees and I wrap it around me. I take a moment to inhale the smell of his shirt, smiling as I look back at his sleeping body. He brought in my crutches, and I grab one of them to lean against as I hop out of the room.

I hobble to the living room and see the dying embers of last night's fire in the wood stove. I open the glass door and poke at the embers, sticking another log on top of them with some old newspaper. I watch as the paper catches fire and the new log starts to burn. I stand and watch the log burn, feeling the warmth of the fire seep through to my bones.

I turn toward the small kitchen and see a coffee maker. It looks well-used, and it only takes me a few moments to find the coffee and put a pot on. Soon, the smell of fresh coffee is filling the small cabin. I lean against the counter and look around the room.

This is where Aiden has lived for who-knows-how-many years. Two small rooms with an outdoor shower. One sofa, one wood-burning stove, and a small kitchen.

This is the exact opposite of my luxury apartment in New York. The coffee machine gurgles behind me for a couple more minutes until I take out a mug and pour myself a cup. I bring the cup up to my nose and inhale the fresh scent of coffee, closing my eyes to enjoy this simple pleasure.

"You're up early," Aiden's gravelly voice makes me jump. I open my eyes and see him emerging from the bedroom. His eyes scan the room, taking in the new fire and the fresh pot of coffee. "I'm used to waking up alone, but I was hoping to wake up next to you."

A smile drifts onto my face as he takes a step closer to me. He leans down and places a soft kiss on my lips. When he stands up, his eyes are soft and he runs his finger along my cheek.

"I made coffee," I say, nodding to the pot. Aiden smiles and nods.

"Not used to having a woman around," he says with a grin.

"Don't get any ideas," I respond, elbowing him in the ribs. "I'm a career woman, remember?"

"A career woman who's wearing my shirt and looks incredibly sexy standing in my kitchen," he growls. He leans over to kiss me again and all the worries from this morning evaporate. With Aiden next to me, all I feel is peace and contentment, and that familiar spark between my legs.

I WRAP my arms around Maddy and hold her tight against me. Ever since I found her in the woods, I don't want to let her out of my sight. I hardly know the woman, but I'm drawn to her in a way that I've never felt before. I pull away and kiss her one more time, lifting her up so she's sitting on the kitchen counter in front of me. She makes the sexiest little giggle as I lift her up, and she wraps her arms around my neck.

"How's the ankle this morning?" I ask.

She shrugs. "It's fine. Better. Still might be a couple days before I can walk right." She grins at me. "But that might have something to do with last night as well."

A growl passes through my chest and I bring my lips to hers again. Her lips taste like the sweetest strawberries, and every time I look at her, I just want to press them to mine. She slips her tongue into my mouth and I groan, pressing my body against hers. I wrap my arms around her waist and slide her forward until she's on the edge of the countertop. She melts into me, kissing me harder and tangling her fingers into my hair. I groan as my cock starts to pulse between my legs. Anytime she's near, I can hardly control myself.

I pull away from her and run my finger along her jaw. "What's bothering you?" I whisper.

Her face contorts and she looks away. Her eyes get a distant look in them and her brows knit together. She shakes her head slightly and takes a deep breath.

"I feel like I don't know myself anymore. I've spent so much time trying to make my own way." She pauses and looks back at me. "My father owns a company, and it was always expected that I'd go and work for him. Pursuing environmental engineering was a big deal. It's been my entire identity since I was a teenager. I've always been the tree-hugging daughter of the oil and gas tycoon."

I try to keep my face steady as she takes another deep, raking breath. She looks at me again and shakes her head.

"Ever since I've come here..." She pauses, putting her hand on my chest. "Ever since I saw you speak at that town hall meeting, everything seems like it's crumbling down. I don't know who I am anymore. Dad is sick, and I don't know if I'm doing the right thing, and – "

Maddy's voice breaks and her face scrunches as she brings her hands up to hide it. I stroke her arm, opening my mouth to speak but not knowing what to say.

"Maddy..." I say slowly. She drops her hand and shakes her head.

"This is embarrassing. I'm sorry. I hardly even know you. I don't know why I'm telling you all this." She lifts her face up to mine and I see the pain in her eyes. I want to ask her about her dad, ask her about her life, but she shakes her head.

"I went up the mountain to try to figure all this out. I've been going into work and doing all the things I've done for years, but suddenly it feels fake. I was walking, looking at these forests and thinking I'm making a mistake."

I nod, feeling my heart grow in my chest as she speaks. I thought she was one of them, one of those corporate vampires that just feed off small towns like Lang Creek. But the look on her face – it's so genuine. She *gets* it. She gets the power of the mountains and she understands how precious they are.

Maddy takes another deep breath and lifts her eyes up to me. Her eyebrows draw together. "Do you hate me? Do you hate me for being one of them?"

I shake my head. "I don't think I could hate you. Even the fact that you're thinking all these things makes me think more of you than I can say."

She nods slowly and I see tears gathering in her eyes. I want to comfort her. I want to tell her that it's okay, but what can I say? On Monday she'll go back to her job and the hotel will be built. In a few months, she'll leave. I've only known her a couple weeks; I can't ask her to change her whole life just because she's spent a bit of time walking in the woods. I move my hand up and down her thigh and clear my throat.

"What's wrong with your dad?" I ask. She flicks her eyes up to me and then back down. She shakes her head from side to side.

"He's sick."

There's a finality to her words, and I can tell she doesn't want to talk about it. My chest feels heavy and I open my mouth. I want to tell her about my dad, about how he raised us and how he died, but the words won't come out. Mara McCoy's face flashes through my mind and the black anger in my heart starts to grow.

I look back at Maddy and wrap my hands around her waist, giving her a gentle squeeze.

"You just have to figure out what you believe in," I say. "And follow that."

A tear rolls down her cheek and I worry that I've said the wrong thing. It was a stupid thing to say anyway, it's just a platitude that doesn't mean anything. I open my mouth again but she speaks first.

"What if what I believe in is exactly the opposite of what I'm doing? Even if I walk away, the hotel will still be built. They'll get someone else to do the paperwork I do and the corporation will still make their money. And plus, if I walk away then my career is finished. Everything I've worked for years to build will be gone." She takes a deep breath and rises a bit straighter, brushing her eyes and forcing a smile.

"I'm sorry. You want some coffee?"

I nod my head, ignoring the lump in my throat. She hops down from the counter and hobbles to the coffee machine. She pours me a mug of coffee and grabs her own and I can tell from her face that our conversation is over. Our fingers brush against each other when she hands me the mug, and her eyes linger on mine for a moment. The depth of her pain is obvious to me and all I want to do is make it go away.

She hops toward me and puts a hand on my shoulder. She kisses my cheek and pulls away, smiling gently at me.

"Thank you for saving me," she says with a smile. "And for listening to my quarter-life crisis."

I chuckle and press my lips to hers. She tastes like coffee, and I open my mouth to kiss her deeper. When I pull away, I tuck her hair behind her ear and smile at her.

"I'd listen to you all day long," I say. I nod to the fire. "Let's sit over there. We can watch the sun come up from the couch. It's what I've done every morning for the past ten years," I admit. She smiles.

"I'd love to."

25

MADELINE

I HOBBLE into the site office on my crutches and get exactly the greeting I've been expecting. A healthy mix of concern and laughter erupts as I walk in. I nod and smile and roll my eyes. Barry comes up to my desk and nods at my ankle.

"Everything okay?"

"Just a bit of a sprain. Should be okay in a couple days," I respond. He nods again and I take a deep breath. Usually I feel completely at ease around Barry, but these days it feels tense. I think he can sense my reluctance on the project.

"Have you finished those applications we spoke about last week? For the sports complex on the north side of the hotel?"

I gulp and shake my head. "Not yet, sorry Barry. I'll have them done by the end of the day."

Barry's face sours and I know he isn't happy with me. He nods curtly and gets up again, heading toward his desk. The site offices are small and simple, just a few portables in the woods. I have one steel-toed boot on my good leg, and I slide my bright high-vis vest on over my jacket.

I glance around the office at the engineers, surveyors, project managers, and I wonder if any of them feel the way I do. Do any of them think what we're doing is wrong? Do any of them see the beauty of the mountains and forests and animals around us?

I turn to see one of the engineers laughing with a construction supervisor and the sound grates on my ears. It doesn't seem like anyone cares. They love driving the big machines and cutting down trees. They like digging holes and pouring concrete.

They like destroying these pristine, virgin forests that the people of Lang Creek have called home for generations.

I shake my head. I can't think like that. My coworkers aren't bad people. I'm not a bad person. Before I came to Lang Creek, I worked on countless projects that would have had the same impact on the environment, or worse. I never gave it a second thought.

Cecilia drops a mug of coffee on my desk and smiles at me. "You alright? You look a little worse for wear today. I didn't see you at the community garden yesterday."

That's because I was busy having sex with Aiden all weekend.

"Just the ankle," I respond. "Took it easy this weekend."

Cecilia nods. She searches my face again and frowns. "Are you okay?"

I nod, maybe a bit too vigorously. "I'm fine. Thanks for the coffee. I should probably get cracking on this application for the sports complex, Barry didn't seem too happy that it was late."

Cecilia nods and stares at my face for a few moments longer. She finally leaves my desk and I turn back to my computer, letting out a long sigh.

Ever since this project started, it's been harder and harder to fake my way along. I just don't have the drive or the belief that we're doing the right thing, and it makes it almost impossible to do my job.

I shift in my seat and my ankle throbs. I wince. It's like a constant physical reminder of the weight on my shoulders. Maybe spraining my ankle was a sign that I shouldn't be here.

The application for the sports complex is started, and I get to work completing it. I work diligently, trying to minimize the impact the complex will have on the surrounding areas. I make sure to include extra environmental controls and extra barricades for the public in the diagrams for the application. I classify the development more strictly than we'd first discussed. I glance up at Barry, knowing the additions will cost the company thousands once they're approved by the Department.

At least if I'm here, working for this company, I can do my best to minimize our impact.

The day goes by and I finish the application, with all the extra controls. I send it over to Barry and use my crutches to walk over to his desk.

"That application is done now, so I'll send it through whenever you've approved it."

"Just send it, Maddy. I've worked with you long enough to trust your work."

My chest squeezes as I think of all the additions I've made. It's a drop in the bucket for the company, but it still feels wrong to deceive Barry. I hobble back to my desk and send the application through to submit it. I let out a big sigh and lean back in my chair.

My head is a mess. I don't know what the right thing to do is. I'm still working for this construction company, so I'm still complicit in the destruction of the forest. Now I'm not doing my job well, because I'm costing my own company thousands in extra environmental controls.

Maybe I should just quit. If I quit, then someone else will take over and at least I won't have it on my conscience. Just as the thought crosses my mind, a text comes through on my phone. It's Aiden, and I unlock my phone to see a photo of the mountains from the viewpoint where he took me the first day.

I stare at the photo and my heart squeezes in my chest. If I quit, then I have to go back to New York. There's nothing for me here, but I'm not yet ready to leave Aiden. I feel drawn to him in a way that I've never felt drawn to a man before.

If I quit, I'm being true to myself but I'm giving up my chance to be with this complex, understanding, gentle, strong, beautiful man. I'll be leaving right as we're starting to get to know each other.

I send a quick text back, asking to meet him tonight. I can't imagine sleeping on my own again, not after spending the weekend in his arms. When I got back to the hotel this morning, Margaret McCoy gave me a loaded look. I know if I'm away for more than a few nights she'll start asking questions, but right now I can't be bothered to care.

I want to see Aiden. With my career such a head wreck, the construction of the hotel so conflicting, and with my dad sick, Aiden is the only thing that feels right anymore. When I'm with him, it feels like things might work out.

My shoulders relax and a smile drifts across my face when he answers my text.

Obviously I want to meet up tonight. Pick you up at the hotel at 7.

My heart jumps in my chest and I smile a bit wider. Even with everything else falling to pieces around me, Aiden is my anchor in the storm. I know that he's a good person, and maybe if I spend time with him, I'll figure out how to make sense of everything.

26

AIDEN

THIS TIME when I drive my father's old truck into town, I don't feel nervous. I drive straight to the McCoy hotel and I don't care who sees me. It doesn't matter who says what, who talks about me, what they say. It doesn't matter that Mara McCoy ripped my family apart and her family stole our livelihood. None of that matters, because a beautiful woman called Madeline Croft wants to see me.

When I'm with her, all the pain that I've clung on to seems to ease. I actually *want* to spend time with her, to be in the company of another human. All day today, all I could think about was her laugh, and the way her nose scrunches when she thinks something's funny. When she's laughing really hard, she doesn't make any noise at all.

I pull up outside the hotel and jump out as Maddy emerges from the front door, kicking the door open with a crutch and making her way toward me. She's wearing tight jeans and a shirt with a light sweater over it, and she looks amazing. She could wear anything and she'd look incredible. When I woke up and saw her in my shirt on Saturday morning, I thought it was the sexiest thing I'd ever seen.

We hardly say a word to each other as I help her into the truck. I see some movement in the hotel window, and I smile to myself. That'll be Margaret McCoy, keeping an eye on everything that's going on. By the end of the night, everyone will know that Maddy got into my truck.

I jump in behind the steering wheel and look at Maddy. "You know that you'll be the talk of the town, right? Are you sure you want to be seen with me?"

Maddy grins and my cock starts to pulse. "I'm sure," she says. "Maybe they'll fire me and it'll solve all my problems."

"Except the hotel being built," I say. Her face falls and I immediately regret my words.

"True," she says, shifting her gaze to look out the window. I grimace and start driving the truck. I take a deep breath and try again. I'm not used to speaking to anyone, let alone a beautiful woman who wants to spend time with me.

"I didn't mean that," I say. "I know that you care."

She smiles sadly and nods. "So where are we going?" she asks to change the subject. I grin.

"It's a surprise. I used to go up here all the time when I was a kid." I look over at her as we drive out of the town. The sun is starting to go down and everything has a golden glow. She glances over at me and laughs, exactly how I was imagining it all day long.

"Keep your eyes on the road," she laughs. "I already have a sprained ankle. I don't want to end up dead."

"I can't help it that you're so beautiful," I say. The words fall out of my mouth and I'm not sure if I'm blushing more or if she is. She smiles at me again and turns to look out the front of the truck. After a few moments she runs her hand along the dash.

"I like this truck," she says.

"It was my father's," I reply. She glances over at me and I keep my eyes facing forward.

"Did he die?" she asks.

It's my turn to feel my throat close up and I can tell she feels bad for her question. I nod my head up and down a couple times and try to open my mouth to speak. My voice comes out as a croak, so I clear my throat and try again.

"There was an accident," I explain. "He died a long time ago, down near the river at the end of town."

Maddy's hand slides over my thigh and she squeezes my leg gently. She says nothing, but I know that she understands. I want to tell her the whole story, how Mara was taunting me, how she fell, how he tried to save her. But if I tell her that, I have to tell her what the McCoys did to my brothers and me afterward, and I can't bear to think about it. That black hole in my heart is still filled with anger and I'm not ready to let it go.

Her hand moves back and forth along my leg and I feel my shoulders relax. Slowly, my jaw unclenches and I take a deep breath.

"I'm sorry," she says. "That's awful. Your mom...?"

"Died when I was young. Cancer."

"Aiden..." she breathes.

"It was hard," I respond. We drive in silence until I turn off and start winding my way up the mountain. There's a lookout just off the road, close enough for Maddy to walk to with crutches. On a clear night like tonight, we'll be able to lay under the stars and see thousands of them twinkling back at us. We drive the rest of the way without saying anything, until I pull over and kill the engine.

"Come on," I say. "I'll help you."

I grab the basket of food I prepared and the two blankets under one arm, putting my other arm around Maddy's waist. She uses one crutch to make her way down the hard path toward the edge of the cliff. I hear her take a sharp intake of breath as she looks out across the mountains. She finally turns toward me with bright eyes.

"This is incredible," she breathes.

I smile. "These mountains are full of places like this." I spread out the blanket and help her get settled. I pop open a bottle of wine and pour two glasses before jogging back to the truck for some firewood. In a few minutes, I've got a small fire burning beside us, we have wine and I pull out some chicken sandwiches. I hand her one and grin.

"Nothing fancy," I say. She laughs and shakes her head.

"Doesn't need to be fancy. This is so perfect," she says. I lean forward and kiss her gently. The last time I was up here was years ago. It feels good to show her my home, to show her all these places where I've grown up and grown into the man I am. I put my arm around her shoulders and she leans her head against my chest. She sighs and snuggles into me, lifting her chin up toward the sky.

"This is incredible, Aiden," she breathes. "Thank you."

A lump forms in my throat and all I can do is nod. I know that she works for the hotel, and once it's built then all this will change. People will find all these little spots that have been almost sacred to the people of Lang Creek. I know that once the hotel is built, Maddy will be gone. I know all those things but I still can't help but feel lucky to be here with her. The black hole in my heart seems to be shrinking with every minute that we spend together.

She turns her head toward me and runs her fingers along my jaw to grip the nape of my neck. She pulls my lips toward hers and kisses me tenderly, wrapping her arm around me and letting me taste those sweet lips once again. I take the wine glass from her hands and put it to the side, pulling her down on top of me. She giggles as we fall backward, letting her hand rest on my chest as she stares into my eyes.

"Thank you, Aiden, for showing me this. For showing me that there's more to life than what I thought before. I feel like a different person than I was a few weeks ago. I don't know how to explain it."

I don't know what to answer, because I feel the same way. How can I put into words that for the first time in years, it feels like there's a reason for me to be here? There's a reason for me to live? I can't put words together so I just tilt my head up and taste her lips again. We forget our wine, forget my simple chicken sandwiches and make love under the blanket of stars above us. I run my hands over her body and feel her shudder and shake as she comes. I watch the ecstasy pass over her face under the moonlight, surrounded by the forests where I've lived my whole life. My whole body releases and I come with her, the two of us locked in this moment of bliss with nothing to think about except each other.

27

———

MADELINE

WHEN AIDEN DROPS me off at the hotel again, I feel like I'm on a high. He helps me out of the car and sets me on my crutches before standing in front of me with his eyes soft and a smile floating over his lips.

"I really want to kiss you right now," he says, "but I know that it would just cause you trouble in town."

I raise an eyebrow. "Trouble?"

He nods to the streets around us. "People talk. Especially them," he says, nodding toward the McCoy hotel. I look from the big hundred-year-old timber building back to him. I smile.

"Thing is, Aiden," I say slowly, dragging my eyes up to his and shifting my weight on my crutches. "I don't give a shit."

A grin splits his face open and he shrugs before tucking his finger under my chin. His lips crush against mine and he kisses me hard, wrapping his hand around my head and

153

pulling me into him. When we pull apart, I brush my hair from my forehead and smile.

"See you tomorrow?" I ask.

He nods and I smile, my heart thumping against my ribcage as I head toward the hotel. I'm as giddy as a teenager, swinging along my crutches and trying not to fall.

There's some movement in the top window, a curtain moving or someone at the window. A chill goes down my spine and I frown, looking back over my shoulder to see Aiden driving away. His father's old truck disappears down the road, back toward his little cabin in the mountains. I glance back at the window where I saw the movement, but it's completely still. With a deep breath, I make it to the front door.

It swings open before I can reach it, and Margaret McCoy's hawk-like features greet me in the entrance. She stares at me for a moment before stepping aside and holding the door open for me.

"Did you have a nice evening?" she croons. I resist the urge to give her a loaded look. I force myself to smile and I nod my head.

"It was lovely, thanks. The weather is warmer than I thought it would be."

"Mm," she says. I shuffle my way toward the steps and take them one at a time, hopping up with my crutches under one arm.

I can't wait for this ankle to heal. I can feel Margaret's eyes on my back with every step. It's not until I turn the corner at the top of the stairs that I let out a sigh of relief. I make my way to my room and kick the door closed with my crutch. I lean the crutches against the wall and sit down on the edge of my bed. My heart is racing and I'm starting to sweat from the exertion of coming up the stairs.

There's a knock on the door and I frown. The person knocks again, a little bit harder this time.

"Madeline," I hear through the door. It's Cecilia's voice. I sigh. I don't feel like talking to her right now, but I call her in anyway.

"Come in, Cecilia," I say. "It's unlocked."

She shuffles in and closes the door behind her before turning toward me and shaking her head.

"Madeline, what are you thinking?" she starts. I sit up a bit straighter, surprised at her tone of voice.

"What do you mean?" I ask, my voice hard.

"You can't go around kissing the townspeople! We're supposed to be professionals here! Don't you remember the code of conduct training that we signed?"

"Cecilia, right now I don't really give a shit. What difference does it make? It's my personal time and my personal life. We're living in this town for the next six months, and if I meet someone I like, what's the problem?"

Cecilia takes a step toward me and wrings her hands. She stares at my face and shakes her head.

"The problem is that Aiden Clarke is the main opposition to the construction of the hotel that *we* are building! And haven't you heard the stories about him and his brothers?"

I frown. I haven't heard any stories, but then again, I haven't asked about them either. Cecilia is much better at extracting gossip and information from everyone around her. She takes another step toward me and pulls out the chair next to the wall. She sits across from me and leans forward.

"Years ago, Danny Clarke - the father - died in an accident. The brothers went nuts. Dominic, the oldest, had to be arrested. They got *violent*, Madeline. All three of them."

She pauses, wringing her hands again and looking at me.

"Is that really who you want to be associated with? And with them opposing the construction of the hotel... Madeline, do you really know what his intentions are?"

I take a deep breath. I'm not ready to believe her. Not after the evening I just had. The way Aiden touched me was in no way violent. It was tender and loving and beautiful. I lift my eyes up to her.

"Who told you this?"

"Margaret told me a couple weeks ago, when Aiden Clarke came down to the community garden. I've been meaning to tell you but I didn't think you were *involved*."

I bristle. I don't know why, but I don't trust Margaret McCoy. After what Aiden told me, that the McCoys stabbed his family in the back when his father died, it sounds like there's a lot going on that we don't know about.

"Madeline, even without the hotel, even without the stories, do you really want to get yourself in the middle of this mess?"

Cecilia's face is earnest, and for the first time I nod to agree.

"No," I concede. "I know it's not a good idea to get in the middle of small town drama. Especially since we work for the company building the biggest hotel this place has ever seen."

"Especially when our main support is coming from the McCoys, who will also be part owners in the new hotel."

My eyes flick up to Cecilia and I frown. "What?"

Cecilia's eyebrows shoot up toward her hairline and she nods. "I saw the contract on Barry's desk the other day when I was looking for the community liaison report. The McCoys will own twenty percent of the new hotel."

"That explains their support," I say. "I thought they were just wanting more tourism in the area. Why would that be kept quiet?"

Cecilia shrugs. "Probably small-town politics. There's so much opposition to the construction that they don't want to seem opportunistic."

"But that's exactly what they are," I spit. Cecilia frowns and nods. She glances toward the door and shakes her head.

"I don't know, Madeline. It seems messy. I don't think you should be seeing that man anymore, but it's not my decision to make."

Her face is drawn and for the first time I see a bit of motherliness in her. I think this conversation is coming from a place of real concern. I think she really cares about me. I nod my head, chewing on her words as I try to process all this information.

"I'll be careful," I say. "No more kissing in town," I laugh.

Cecilia snorts and shakes her head. "That would be a start."

"Was it you that was looking at us through the window? I saw some movement in the top corner room."

She frowns and looks toward the door. She shakes her head. "No, my room faces the back of the hotel. I heard you coming up the stairs. Stomping up like a baby elephant with those things," she grins, nodding at the crutches.

I chuckle as she gets up to leave. A current of worry passes through me. If it wasn't her watching me through the curtains, who was it?

Cecilia nods at me one more time and walks out of my room. I hop over to the bathroom and start getting ready for bed. My head is spinning and I don't know what to think. She's right, it's not good to get in the middle of small town problems.

But then I think of Aiden, and how he makes me feel happier than I've felt in years, and I don't know what to do. I climb into bed, alone this time. It feels cold and lonely without his arms around me. As I drift off to sleep, I know that I won't be able to stay away from him, even if I wanted to.

28

AIDEN

WHEN I GET BACK to the cabin, there's another pickup in the driveway. It's Sheriff Whittaker's truck. He's sitting in the front seat with the engine running, waiting for me. I pull up beside him and turn my engine off, jumping out and circling toward his vehicle. He gets out of his own truck and extends his hand for me to shake.

"Bill," I say. "What can I do for you? Hope you haven't been waiting long."

"Couple minutes," he says. "Can I come in?"

"Sure," I respond. Our feet crunch on the gravel as we make our way to the tiny cabin that I call home. I let him in and head for the wood stove, lighting it before facing the Sheriff again. I nod to the table.

"Coffee?"

"Sure," he says, taking a seat at my small round table. I put some coffee on and head back toward the table. I sit across from the Sheriff and study his face. He looks almost worried. He's staring at me steadily, but there's something in his eyes that I don't recognize.

"So what's going on?"

"Aiden, I don't know how to tell you this," he starts. He looks down at his hands and takes a deep breath. I frown as my heart starts to beat a bit harder.

"What's wrong? Is it Dominic? Is he in trouble? Is it Ethan? His Ranger training?"

He shakes his head from side to side and my shoulders relax. "No, no, no. Nothing like that. As far as I know your brothers are fine."

I nod my head slowly as the coffee machine gurgles behind me. I get up to pour a couple of mugs as Bill composes himself. He doesn't look ready to talk, and as much as I want him to spit it out, I get up to give him a moment's space.

The two mugs of coffee slosh as I set them down on the table. Bill nods in appreciation and grabs one of them, taking a long drink before looking at me again.

"It's the girl, Aiden. The environment girl."

"Maddy?" I say, frowning. Bill nods. My heart starts to beat a bit faster and my eyes harden as I look at him. "She's a woman, first of all. An environmental engineer. Not an 'environment girl'."

Bill looks at me and then back at his mug, nodding. "Right, sorry," he says. He takes a deep breath and looks back at me. "Aiden, you have to stop seeing her."

"Like fuck I do," I spit back at him. The anger is starting to flood my veins as I stare at him in front of me. How dare he come into my house and tell me what to do in my own personal time. Does he think that because he's Sheriff that he gets to decide who I can date?

Bill takes a deep breath and shakes his head again. "Aiden, the townspeople are looking to you for guidance. They listened to you at the town hall meeting. There's another meeting being called for next week. We're going to petition the state government to block the construction. Will you sign it?"

I stare at him for a few moments and nod my head slowly. "Yes," I answer. I might not want to be the spokesman they want but I still don't want the hotel to be built.

Bill nods and takes a deep breath. "Great, thanks. But Aiden, if you're speaking publicly against it, and then getting into bed with one of the company workers..." His voice trails off and he finally lifts his eyes back up to me. "It doesn't look good."

The anger inside me is starting to feel red hot. I take a deep breath to calm myself down and force my voice to stay steady and low.

"Bill, you're the one who asked me to speak at that meeting, remember? *You* forced that on *me*. *You're* asking *me* to sign this fucking petition. And now you're telling me that I'm not the perfect little poster boy that you were wanting? Are you fucking kidding me?"

"So what, now you want this monstrosity to be built? You want these mountains to be overrun and destroyed by tourists, filled with trash and trampled by people? Is that what you want? Is that what your father would want?"

"Don't fucking talk about my father," I respond. The two of us stare at each other across the tiny table. Our chests are heaving up and down and our eyes are locked together. I hang on to the anger that's coursing through me, not wanting to let go of it when he's telling me how to live my life.

Bill backs down first. He slumps back in his chair and brings his hand to his forehead. He shakes his head slowly from side to side and my heartbeat starts to slow. When he speaks, his voice is calmer.

"Aiden, I know I asked a lot of you. I know I'm still asking a lot of you. The McCoys are pushing hard for this hotel to be built, and I don't know why yet. I can't figure it out. It can't just be to get more tourists through the town."

"Well I wouldn't trust them," I snarl. "They stole my father's businesses right after they fucking killed him."

Bill looks at me and says nothing. We stare at each other for a few long moments until he raps his knuckles on the table and stands up.

"I'm trying to figure this out, Aiden. I'm just asking for a bit of help. This hotel won't benefit anyone except the McCoys, and they have too much pull around here already. Sometimes I wonder if this uniform means anything anymore."

I take a deep breath and Bill looks at me one more time.

"Can you just cool it off with your woman? Don't be so public about it? Just until I figure this out? Until I know what's going on and we get this petition off to the state."

Reluctantly, I nod my head. Bill's lips draw into a thin line and he nods back at me.

"Thank you." He walks to the front door and turns back toward me. He takes a deep breath and looks me up and down. "You know, Aiden, I see a lot of your father in you. I respected him and I respect you. It was terrible what happened. You boys deserved better. This could be your chance to make it right. It could be your chance to show the McCoys that they don't run this town, and they don't own any of us."

His words pass through my chest like an arrow and my eyes start to prickle. I say nothing, and he lets himself out of the cabin. When I hear his truck turn down the mountainside, I let out a long breath.

Maybe he's right. Maybe this is my chance to take back my life and livelihood from the McCoys. If there is more going on with them and the new hotel, my being with Maddy is playing directly into their hand.

That familiar hatred for the McCoys blooms in my stomach and I enjoy the feeling of it for a few moments. It's not until Maddy's face paints itself in my mind's eye that I hesitate. For the first time in years, I feel something other than numbness and anger. I feel almost happy when I'm with her.

And now I'm supposed to throw it all away? I'm supposed to let that go for some decades-old feud between our two families?

Even as the thought crosses my mind, I know it's not just a feud between our families. The future of Lang Creek and these mountains hangs in the balance. I lean back in my chair and take a deep breath.

I don't know what to do. I need to choose between my own happiness and my father's legacy. I need to choose between my past and my future, and I don't know which is the right choice.

29

MADELINE

When I wake up, my ankle looks a bit better. The swelling has gone down and I swing my legs over the side of the bed. I stand up, trying to put a bit of weight on my bad foot. To my surprise, pain doesn't shoot through my leg when I lean on it. I take a hesitant step toward the bathroom and smile as I hobble toward the door.

With my ankle feeling better, it might only be a few more days of hobbling and then I'll be back to normal. I decide to leave my crutches at home today. I check my phone and my heart sinks a tiny bit when I see it blank. I shake my head. I'm being silly. Of course Aiden wouldn't text me right away. He's probably busy, either at work or out on the mountain. He's not exactly the texting type.

I hum to myself as I get ready. It doesn't take long until I'm ready for work and heading out to site. I check my phone again and resist the urge to text him. Maybe Cecilia is right. Maybe I should cool it a bit with Aiden, or at least try to be a bit more subtle.

The thought of sneaking around seems wrong. I don't want to sneak around with him. I'm proud of spending time with him. He's the most caring, understanding, complex man I've ever met. I try to push these thoughts aside as I drive into work. I'll need to focus on this hotel for the rest of the day, and not let my thoughts of Aiden or my doubts about the project stop me from doing my job.

Around noon, my phone finally buzzes and my heart jumps when I see Aiden's name. Cecilia looks over at me from across the tiny site office and gives me a knowing look. I ignore her and type a reply. I can't keep the smile from my face - I'll see him again tonight.

The afternoon drags on, and I end up staring at my computer screen without getting anything done for what seems like an eternity. I try to focus on the environmental reports that I need to prepare, and on making sure all our applications are up to date. I try to focus on the daily inspections I do on the site but all I can think of is Aiden. I keep seeing his face in my mind and imagining what his hands feel like when they're on my body.

This time, I'll drive out to meet Aiden at his place. At least we won't be seen together there.

After a few hours that last a lifetime, I finally drive away from the construction site. I leave the dust and dirt and timber and barricades and high-vis clothing in my rear-view mirror. I drive back to the hotel and hobble up to my room to shower, rushing to get back in my car and drive out of town.

I drive past the 'Welcome to Lang Creek' sign and past the bends in the road that are becoming more familiar with each passing day. I turn off toward Aiden's cabin and smile as my car starts snaking its way up the mountainside. When I turn the engine off, his front door opens and he greets me with arms wide open and a smile painted across his face.

"You made it!"

I laugh. "Did you think I wouldn't?"

"I was worried about your ankle."

"It's feeling much better," I say. It's only half true – it was feeling great this morning but with all the walking I've been doing it's starting to throb. Aiden smiles and wraps his arms around me.

"Thanks for driving up here," he says. "I have to admit I got a stern talking-to about being seen with you in town."

"You did? So did I!" I laugh. "Apparently people don't like seeing us together."

"Apparently not," he says with a grin, sliding his hands toward the small of my back and pulling me into him. He smells like smoke and fresh pine and I take a deep breath before tilting my chin up toward him. His kiss tastes as good as it did yesterday – as good as it did the first day, and as good as I hope it'll taste tomorrow and the next day too. When we pull apart, I glance around at the forest surrounding his cabin and smile.

"It's so peaceful up here," I say. "I understand why you live here."

Aiden grunts in response and puts his arm around my waist to guide me to the cabin. When we get a bit closer, I see something through the trees. It looks like a building of some sort.

"What's that?" I ask, pointing to the building. "It looks like a big house!"

"It is a house," he says. I glance up at his face and see it darken. "We used to live there, before the accident."

He guides me toward the cabin and I glance up toward the big house one more time. I can sense that Aiden doesn't want to talk about it, so I let him lead me inside. We sit on the couch together. He brings me a beer. We laugh, we talk, we make love. His touch feels even better than it did before. It feels like we're starting to get to know each other's bodies in a way that I didn't think was possible. Every time he touches me it feels more intimate than the last time. Every time I come, it feels more intense – like my body is letting go of just a little bit more tension with every orgasm he gives me.

The sun has gone down and the moon is shining in the night sky when I finally sigh. Aiden's arm is draped over my shoulders, and my naked body is pressed against his under the blankets of his bed. I look up at him and smile sadly.

"I should go," I say. "I need to work tomorrow."

"Don't go," he says, wrapping his arm around me. I chuckle and lay a soft kiss on his lips.

"I don't want to," I say. He smiles and kisses me again.

"I'll drive behind you to the main road," he says. "To make sure you make it down safely."

My heart grows in my chest and I smile at him. He's so attentive, so thoughtful that it constantly surprises me. How could this be the violent brute of a man that Cecilia was telling me about? How could this be a man who needs a warning?

When we get to the main road, he flashes his headlights at me and I wave at him through the window. I watch his headlights in the mirror as I drive back toward town, sad to be leaving but happy to be with him.

WE SPEND the next few weeks exactly like that. On weeknights, we steal any time together we can. On weekends we take off together and he shows me the mountains where he grew up. Every day, I get to see a little bit more of him and I feel myself falling for him. I've never met anyone as beautiful as him. He makes me feel like I matter, like he sees me for who I am and not for who he wants me to be. For those weeks, I don't think about the hotel, or the environment, or my father. I'm just completely, blissfully happy.

30

———

AIDEN

MADDY'S GONE AGAIN, and I turn back toward the empty cabin. It always feels colder and darker after she leaves. I wish she would stay with me every night, but I know why she doesn't. It's not like it's a secret that we're together - I'm pretty sure everyone in town knows. It would be a long drive from here to site every day for her, and I know she doesn't want to be late for work.

I slump down on the sofa and watch the fire crackling in the stove. These past few weeks have flown by without me realizing. Every day I have something to look forward to, knowing that I'll see Maddy that night. Every night, I have the memory of her body next to mine to help me fall asleep.

It feels almost like happiness. Is this what happiness feels like? It's almost like I feel lighter than I did before. I don't cling on to things that bother me. The air tastes sweeter than it did before. Maybe that's summer, or maybe it's Maddy.

I open my eyes when I hear a car coming up the road. There's only one reason a car comes up here, and it's to come to this

171

cabin. I immediately think of Maddy. Is she coming back? Is she in trouble? Did something happen? Does she finally want to sleep over on a work night?

My heart starts to beat a bit faster as I stand up and walk outside. A mixture of relief and disappointment washes over me when I see my brother's truck. He parks outside and both doors open, with my two brothers spilling out of either side.

Dominic grunts and his huge body lumbers toward me. Ethan raises his hand.

"Hey, brother!" he calls out. He's thinner and taller than Dominic and me, with longer hair that falls just over his ears. He's always been more coordinated than Dominic and me, almost graceful. Where Dominic and I are brute strength, he's cleverness. He opens his arms and wraps me in a big bear hug.

"What are you two doing all the way up here?" I ask when we pull apart.

Ethan snorts. "What, three brothers can't visit with each other on a Wednesday night?"

I grin and nod my head toward the cabin. The three of us head inside and suddenly the room feels tiny. Between Ethan's height and Dominic's and my width, there's not much room to move. They sit down on the couch where Maddy and I just made love and I pull up one of my chairs. I pass out beers and we drink the first few gulps in silence.

"So how was the Park Ranger training?" I ask Ethan.

He grins. "It was great. All passed and certified now," he says. He's beaming with pride and I can't help but smile along.

"Congrats, Ethan. You deserve it."

He nods and glances at Dominic. Dominic shifts in his seat and takes a long drink of beer. I can tell they're not here for a friendly chat, and I'm about to find out what they have to say. Ethan clears his throat and looks me in the eye.

"Aiden," he starts. "This hotel."

I put up my hand. "I don't want to hear it," I snip. "You guys are going to have to find some other hero to oppose this thing."

Ethan shakes his head. "That's not why we're here. Look, construction is going fast. Have you been over there lately? The past couple months they've made a lot of progress."

"No," I admit. "I haven't wanted to see it."

Dominic and Ethan exchange another glance and then look back at me. Dominic finally speaks. "I think you should see it."

I look him in the eye and then shift my gaze to Ethan. Both of them are staring at me steadily. As much as I want to tell them to leave, that I don't want to face this thing head on, I know that they're right. I can't keep burying my head in the sand and pretending that Maddy doesn't work for the corporation that's destroying the forests I love. My brothers are right. I need to see it.

I nod my head once. "Okay," I say simply. Dominic grunts in response and Ethan nods. The three of us stand up without another word and we head to Dominic's truck. We drive in silence along the mountain's logging roads. Not many people know their way around these roads, but we've lived here our whole lives. Dominic drives up and up and up until I know we're way above the work site. He turns again and the forest opens up below us. We have a perfect bird's eye view of the darkened construction site.

Dominic kills the engine and the three of us step outside. My throat tightens as I look at the huge swath of land that's been clear-cut. The frame of the hotel is already up, and I can just see partition walls starting to go in. There are dozens of excavators and trucks parked in a neat line down the far end of the site, and the whole area is a mess of mud and logs and materials.

After a few minutes I glance at my brothers, who look at me solemnly.

"It's so much bigger than I thought it would be," I finally say. It's the first time any of us has spoken since my cabin, and my voice sounds too loud in the quiet forest. I look back down on the work site and my eyes start to water. From up here, it doesn't look like construction. It just looks like destruction.

Ethan clears his throat. "Bill found something out yesterday. The McCoys..." his voice trails off and I turn my head toward him.

"What about the McCoys?"

"They own twenty percent of it."

I frown, struggling to understand his words. "Twenty percent of what?"

"Twenty percent of that," he says, sweeping his arm toward the construction site. My blood turns to ice and I follow his arm to look at the hotel once again. "Mara's new husband is the CEO's son."

"So the reason they've been pushing for this..."

"It's exactly what they did to dad's business, except this time they're not waiting for anyone to die."

I look at Ethan and feel my face scrunch up. My stomach feels like it's full of lead, and my heart feels like it's going to explode. This whole hotel construction – the entire development... it was all the McCoys? The weight of it seems too much. I can't deal with it. I can't understand it, and I can't process it. I can't do anything except feel the black anger fill my heart as I stare down at the site below me.

"What do you want me to do?" I ask. "What can we do? There's nothing. It's too late. Look at it, it'll be done in a few months."

And then Maddy will leave and I'll have to live with this hotel for the rest of my life.

"We could torch it," Dominic says in the silence. I snort and glance over at my eldest brother.

"Right," I say. "That's legal."

Dominic turns to look at me and shrugs. "Got any better ideas?"

I look back at the huge worksite and take a deep breath. "Let's get out of here," I say. "I can't look at this anymore."

"Aiden, we need your help," Ethan says. The frustration is starting to overwhelm me and I spin around toward him, taking a few steps until our chests are inches apart.

"What the fuck do you want from me! Why does everyone think I can fix this? What do you want me to DO?" My chest is heaving up and down, and I can feel the veins in my neck throbbing with every beat of my heart. Ethan stands his ground in front of me, and Dominic watches us. We stand in silence until I finally sigh and slump my shoulders. I turn toward the truck and open the door.

"Just burn the fucking thing down," I say. "That seems like the only actual solution anyone's had in months."

I see Ethan and Dominic exchange a glance out of the corner of my eye, and then they slide into the truck without a word. We drive back the way we came in silence, and when they pull up outside the cabin, I get out without saying anything. It's not until I hear them drive back down the road away from the cabin that I sit down and put my head in my hands, and let the tears flow freely down my cheeks.

I don't know what to do. I don't know how to fix this. I don't want to let go of Maddy, but this feels like the past repeating itself. They stole dad's business from us and now they just want more. My heart is breaking and I don't know what to do about it.

MADELINE

When I drive into work, I can already tell something is wrong. I see Barry pacing back and forth outside on the phone. His eyebrows are drawn together. I can see that little patch of red skin on his forehead that he only gets when he's really upset. I park my car and get out, and he glances over for a moment before pacing back the other way.

I try not to let the dread set in. Something is definitely wrong. With a deep breath, I walk up to the small site office and slide inside. Just like every other morning, I drop my lunch in the fridge and pour myself a coffee before heading to my desk. I'm just settling in and waiting for my computer to boot up when Barry comes flying through the door.

"Madeline!" he shouts, staring at me across the room. "Conference room. NOW."

My heart starts pounding. I grab a notebook and pen as I get up and head toward the small meeting room at the back of the offices. Barry is not the type to fly off the handle like this.

He's the most level-headed manager I've ever had, and I've only seen him truly angry once or twice before.

I shuffle to the conference room and see Barry sitting at the head of the table with a few documents in front of him. He motions to a seat to his left and I sit down, waiting for him to speak. He takes a deep breath and swings his eyes over to me.

"I just got a call from the secretary at the Department of Environmental Conservation," he starts. He takes another deep breath. "Care to explain this?"

He slides over a stack of papers and my heart sinks when I see the application I submitted a few weeks ago.

"What are all these extra controls? You classed the area as highly sensitive? The original assessment had nothing like that in it! Maddy..." He takes a deep breath and I can tell he's trying to control his voice. "Maddy, what is this?"

I look at the report and take a deep breath. "It's my best assessment of the situation," I say in a level voice. It's true. For the first time, I applied for our permit without downplaying the impact that this development would have. "The report is accurate."

Barry takes a deep breath. His eyes are blazing and I force myself not to squirm. "Maddy," he says again. "There's been a petition by the townspeople of Lang Creek. The petition – along with your report – has made the Department revoke our permit to work."

My eyes widen and my chest suddenly feels hollow. "W-what?"

That's not what I intended. I didn't want to stop the job, I just wanted it to be done in an ethical way! I stare at the table, at the report in front of me and feel my heart beating a little bit harder. Is that true? Am I happy? A part of me is relieved that construction has stopped, but when I see the anger in Barry's eyes I don't know how to feel. This wasn't a great career move.

Barry slides another stack of papers to me. "It's the petition from Lang Creek. They got over five thousand signatures, enough to get the department to listen. Maddy, this is bad." He takes a deep breath. "Every day we stand down from work, we're losing hundreds of thousands of dollars. Our construction program was tight enough already and if we don't get to work there's no way we'll hit our deadlines. This is going to cost us millions."

I can't look at him. My head is in turmoil. I can't ignore the part of me that's happy, but I've worked my way up in this company for the past five years. I don't know where my loyalties lie anymore. I scan the petition and my eyes widen when I see one familiar name, right on the first page.

Aiden Clarke

I rearrange my face and try to keep it steady. My heart starts thumping against my chest and now, added to the confusion and dread in my heart, I feel a hint of betrayal. How could he be spending every day with me and not tell me about this? How could he be one of the first people to sign the petition that might make me lose my job?

I force myself to lift my eyes up to Barry. He's staring at me, gauging my reaction. I take a deep breath and nod my head.

"I should have run the report by you. When you said to submit it, I should have flagged the changes," I say. "I'm sorry for that, it was deceitful." I take another deep breath to steady my voice, staring Barry straight in the eye. "But I'm not sorry for the report. It's accurate, and I'll stand by any of the conclusions I made in it about the state of the area and the impact of the hotel."

Barry bristles, and I keep my eyes on his. The anger flares inside him and the little patch of red skin on his forehead reappears. He nods his head once and opens his mouth to speak.

"Maddy, do you understand the gravity of this situation?"

"Barry, I'm not a fucking idiot," I snap. "I know that this is going to cost the company a lot of money. I know that I made a mistake in not telling you what was in that report. But I had nothing to do with this petition! I can't control what the people of Lang Creek do and don't sign!"

"What about your little boyfriend?" he snarls. "I find it hard to believe that you had nothing to do with this." He brings his finger down onto the petition papers in front of me. My jaw drops open and the outrage starts to crawl up my neck until it feels like my cheeks are on fire.

"Excuse me?" I say, incredulous. "You think I had something to do with this? What exactly are you fucking accusing me of, Barry?"

It's my turn to be furious. I'm glad we're in the conference room, but I know that the whole office will be able to hear what we're saying through the thin partition walls. Right now, I don't give a fuck. I can't believe that he would think I would sabotage the project like that!

"I'm saying *exactly* that. I find it hard to believe that at *exactly* the same time you're submitting a report without telling me that you're changing the classification of the site, a petition is being organized and signed and submitted without you knowing anything about it. You're with him every single night!"

The heart is pumping through my veins. I haven't felt this angry in a long, long time. It's almost intoxicating, and all I can see is that stupid patch of red on Barry's forehead.

"My personal life has nothing to do with this," I say through clenched teeth. "And fuck you for suggesting that I would deliberately sabotage the project! We've worked together for five years, Barry." We stare at each other for a few moments. Neither of us move an inch, and the heat of my anger is almost blinding. I try to keep my voice steady. "You know I wouldn't do anything like that. You know what? Go fuck yourself!"

I stand up, pushing my chair back with my legs so that it topples over behind me. My heart is beating fast and my ankle is starting to throb. I stomp out of the office and climb into my car. Within a few seconds, I'm flying down the highway toward the lonely mountain that Aiden Clarke calls home.

As much as I hate to admit it, Barry is right about one thing. I should have known about this petition. That signature on the front page hurt more than anything else a man has ever done to me. The sting of betrayal mixes with anger and outrage until I'm gripping the steering wheel and racing up the mountain.

I need answers, and Aiden Clarke is the only one that can give them to me.

32

AIDEN

I SPEND a restless night after my brothers drop me off. I toss and turn in bed, unable to get comfortable. The cabin feels too small and too cold, and when I light a fire it becomes too hot and stuffy. Finally, the grey light of dawn starts to come through the window and I sit up.

My body is aching, even though I haven't done anything to make it sore. I've hardly slept and I feel like I've aged ten years overnight. I stretch my neck from side to side and take a deep breath. I stand up and make my way to the shower, standing under the hot stream of water until I feel alive again. By the time I come back inside, the coffee pot is full and I pour the first mug of many today.

I scan the small cabin that I've called home for the past ten years. It seems so small and dark right now. I feel almost claustrophobic being in here. I run my fingers through my hair and throw the coffee down my throat.

My brothers are right. The hotel shouldn't be there. Bill agrees. Most of the town agrees. I think of Mara McCoy's face when she drove up to the cabin a couple weeks ago. At first, I thought she was just back to celebrate her engagement with her family, but now I know that she was here for business. With the new hotel being part-owned by their family, she probably wanted to make sure her piece of the pie was safe. I know how she thinks.

I head outside toward the garage. I've spent too much time wallowing in self-pity up here, alone with my thoughts. It's time for me to take back what's mine.

The big 'McCoy Trucking' logo appears in my head and I see red. I head outside, ready to raise hell in town. They may have stolen my father's business, but they sure as hell aren't ruining the sanctity of these mountains by getting into bed with a hotel corporation. I'm not letting that happen. I'm not sure how I'll stop them, but at least I can try.

As I stomp out of the cabin toward my truck, I see a familiar car pulling up near the cabin. Maddy jumps out with the car still running and comes flying toward me.

"How *dare* you," she spits. I stop in my tracks, frowning as she runs toward me. "How dare you lie to me! You bastard!"

She collides with me, and I catch her wrists as she brings them down toward my chest. Her face is streaked with tears and her whole body is trembling.

"Maddy!" I say. My heart is beating fast. "Maddy, what are you talking about? I never lied to you!"

"The petition! You were one of the first to sign it. You never told me about it! Now I'm in the shit at work and I'm probably going to get fired or demoted or moved." She's staring at me, tears streaming down her face and I can see the pain in her eyes. I frown. The petition…?

I remember now, Bill coming up here and warning me off her. He had me sign the petition and promise to keep my relationship with Maddy more subtle. My eyes widen.

"What are you talking about? I didn't think the petition would actually do anything!"

"So you signed it!" she says. "You signed it and you still fucked me every night. You told me that you agreed it would bring more business to the area! I told you about what I was doing at work, how strict I was being with the environmental reports. I told you everything! And you *lied* to me!"

"I never lied," I growl.

"Lying by omission is still lying," she spits. She yanks her hands away from me, fury blazing in her eyes. I start to feel the anger bubbling in my stomach and I shake my head.

"What did you expect, Maddy? You know I didn't want that fucking thing to be built! You think I wouldn't put my name to that? It doesn't matter how many silt fences you put up, you've still clear-cut seven football fields' worth of land over there! It looks like a war zone!"

"You've seen it?" she frowns, taking a step back. "It's a closed site."

"There's logging roads all through these mountains, Maddy," I say with a sigh. "I grew up driving all over them. You don't know these mountains."

"So you keep reminding me," she says bitterly. The tears are gathering in her eyes and she shakes her head. "I can't believe you. I thought you cared about me. All the times I told you what I was doing at work and you told me I was doing a good job. All that time, you were listening to me thinking I was just a fool."

"That's not true," I say. I'm trying my hardest to keep my voice steady.

"Is this a joke to you? You want to fuck the Enviro girl all the while you're spearheading the campaign to kill this project?"

"Maddy," I say. She takes a step back from me and shakes her head.

"I can't believe you. I told you everything. You've made a fool out of me, Aiden. You're a fucking asshole."

"What choice did I have, Maddy! Short of burning the fucking place down, that petition was the only thing I could do!"

Her eyes blaze and she opens her mouth to speak. Nothing comes out, and the tears start spilling over onto her cheeks. She spins on her heels and slams the door to her car. The wheels skid on the gravel as she turns around and races back down the mountain path. I watch her leave and my chest feels like it's being split open with an axe.

I bring my hands up to my head and press my fingers into my skull. I bend at the hips and let out a yell, screaming into the ground as loud as I can to try to release some of the pressure inside me.

I can't take this anymore! I can't take the pressure and the conflict and the questions! What the fuck did she expect? Of course I don't want it to be built! Of course I'd still be against it! She goes to work every day and she sees what they've done to the forest over there. That forest is hundreds of years old, and they've completely destroyed it! For what! For money! To put money in the fucking McCoy family's pocket.

I grab a rock from the ground and hurl it at the nearest tree. It hits the trunk with a hollow knock and bounces off into the forest. I want to scream again. I want to punch something. I want this all to go away.

Even though I know I'm right about the hotel, watching Maddy drive away makes me sick. Seeing the pain in her eyes makes me want to throw up. Having her angry at me makes me want to go over there and build the fucking hotel myself.

I'm being torn in two completely different directions and I don't know what to do about it. I can't get the image of the site from last night out of my mind, but now all I can see is Maddy's tear-streaked face.

When I found her in the forest, I swore I'd protect her, and the past couple months have been the happiest of my life.

I shake my head when the thought passes through it. They haven't been the happiest of my life. They've been a lie. She's been working for the corporation that's destroying everything I hold dear to me. That's not happiness. That's fake. None of it is real. She can be mad at me all she wants. It doesn't change the fact that she's on the opposite side of a problem that I can't accept. I can't compromise.

The hotel shouldn't be there, and if that means Maddy shouldn't be here either, then that's the way it has to be.

She was nothing but a fling. I got carried away.

I set my jaw and repeat the words to myself over and over. She was a fling. She means nothing. I got carried away. I jump in the truck and drive down the mountain. When I get to the main road, a big 'McCoy Trucking' truck passes me and my heart beats even harder.

I know I'm right about this. I can't let the McCoys carve another piece of this town out for themselves. I owe it to my brothers, and I owe it to my father.

Maddy was a fling.

I ignore the dagger that passes through my heart whenever I say those words, and I focus on the black anger in my heart. I turn the truck in the direction of Lang Creek. I need to pay my brothers a visit.

33

MADELINE

I NEED to pull over onto the shoulder as I drive back toward town. I can't see through my tears, and I know I'll get in an accident if I keep driving. I put my hazard lights on and let the sobs shake my body. I rest my head on the steering wheel and let myself cry and cry and cry.

When I can breathe again, I look through the windshield at the vista in front of me. I'm surrounded by the Adirondacks, by the most beautiful scenery I've ever seen. I've always loved being outdoors, but being here has given me a new appreciation for the wild.

No, that's not true. Being here *with Aiden* has given me a new appreciation for the wild.

As mad as I am that he didn't tell me about the petition, as betrayed as I feel by it, I know deep down that I can't blame him for it. I shouldn't be here. I'm on the wrong side of this fight. He's right about it all. It doesn't matter how many environmental controls we put in. It doesn't matter how stringent the regulations are. We've still cleared acres of virgin forest and are putting a huge, wasteful, luxury hotel in its place.

How can I call myself an environmental engineer after this?

My heart feels like it's breaking for a thousand reasons. I'm crying for Aiden, I'm crying for my job, and I'm crying because I know I've been acting falsely in both my professional life and personal life. I'm crying because I haven't been true to myself.

My father's voice rings in my head and I hear him say it again. *Be true to yourself.* I don't even know who I am! How am I supposed to know what to do? I thought I was an environmentalist, so I pursued environmental engineering. And yet here I am, complicit in the destruction of the environment. I've been lying to myself.

I thought I was a career woman, proud of my hard work and proud of making my own way through the ranks of this industry. And yet here I am, making decisions that directly impact my progression. I lied to my boss and I dated the main opponent for the hotel's construction.

I can't be true to myself, because I don't know who I am.

That seems to sober me up. I sob once more and bring my hands up to my cheeks to wipe the tears away. I'm only crying because I'm mad at myself. Aiden hasn't done anything wrong. He's been true to himself. He's never done anything to contradict who he is. All he's ever done is oppose the construction of the hotel. It feels like he lied to me, but maybe I was just too eager to believe my own lies.

I put the car into gear and start back toward Lang Creek Town. I think of Aiden's face when I confronted him, how it twisted and contorted as I accused him of lying. What am I to him? Why was he seeing me? Do I actually mean anything to him?

I sniffle and try to push the thoughts away as I drive. I need to focus on the road.

Still, every tree, every mountain, every bend in the road makes me think of him. He's shown me so much about these mountains, so much about himself. He's shown me so much about *me*. I don't know who I am or what I'm doing, but at least I realize that now. At least now I know that I don't know.

My heart feels like it's breaking. I mean physically breaking. It's a sharp pain that cracks through my chest, and when I finally pull the car up in front of the hotel, I can't get up the stairs fast enough. I lock myself into my room and let the tears flow from my eyes.

My phone is buzzing and buzzing and I finally wipe my eyes and look at it. It's Barry, and Cecilia, and a few of the engineers at work. I scroll through my missed calls and my heart breaks again when I don't see Aiden's name.

His silence says it all.

I lie back on my bed and take a deep breath. I stormed out of work after being confronted about a mistake. I lied to my boss, or at the very least I misled him. My actions have contributed to the project being brought to a halt.

I haven't exactly been a professional about all this. I've been a petulant child.

Sure, Barry shouldn't have brought Aiden up, but I probably shouldn't have been seeing him in the first place. Not if I was serious about wanting to progress in this company. Not if I was serious about this career.

I scroll through my contacts until I find my father's number. When he answers, my heart breaks all over again and I just wish I was a little girl curled up in his arms.

"Daddy," I sob. "I don't know what to do."

I hate how small my voice is, and I hate having to ask my dad for help, but as soon as he starts asking me what's wrong, his voice lends me a bit of strength.

"What's up Mads? Come on, stop crying. Come on kiddo."

I snort as I try to laugh through my tears. "You haven't called me kiddo in years."

"You're still my kid, Madeline," he says gently. "Come on, tell me what happened."

"There's a boy," I blurt out. "A man, I mean."

My father makes a knowing sound and I can imagine him nodding. His voice is like a hug through the phone, and I lie back in bed, bringing my hand to my eyes.

"His name is Aiden. Dad," my voice catches in my throat. "Dad I think I'm in love with him."

"Oh, Mads," my dad says gently. "I wouldn't wish that on my worst enemy."

I snort again as I try to laugh. "And I messed up at work and now the project is stopped and it's all a big mess and it's my fault."

My father chuckles. "You work for an international construction company on a multi-million dollar project. I can guarantee it's not completely your fault. Tell me what happened."

I take a deep breath and start talking. I tell him everything, from the town hall meeting to the community garden to the beauty of the mountains. I tell him about Aiden, and how he's cared for me and been gentler with me than any man before. I tell him that I don't know who I am anymore, and I don't know what I want. I tell him that I feel like I've been lying to myself this whole time.

He listens to it all. By the end of the conversation my voice is steady and my eyes are dry.

"You'll figure it out, Mads," he says. "Go back to work and fix things with your boss. Tomorrow you can talk to Aiden once you've both calmed down."

I nod. "Okay. Thanks, Dad."

"I love you, kiddo."

I laugh, and this time it actually sounds like a real laugh. "I love you too, Dad. It's nice to talk to you."

"Thanks for calling. Let me know how it all goes."

We hang up and I hold the phone to my chest. I take a long, shuddering breath and sit up. I may be a grown woman, but having a heart-to-heart with my dad has always made me feel better. He's given me the courage to go back to work and own up to my mistakes. Tomorrow, I'll go to Aiden and own up to my mistakes with him.

Once that's done, I'll let the cards fall as they may and deal with whatever comes. My dad is right. I'll figure it all out. I wipe my cheeks one more time and take a deep breath. Time to go back to work.

34

————

AIDEN

WHEN I GET to Ethan's house, I bang on the door until he answers. I barge in past him and pace back and forth in the living room until he clears his throat.

"You all right, Aiden?"

"No! I'm not all right. That fucking hotel is driving me insane." *Maddy being mad at me is driving me insane.* "They've stopped construction because of that petition that Bill started. I don't know, I feel like it's temporary."

Ethan nods and I flop down onto his sofa. I let all the air out of my lungs as Ethan sits across from me and studies my face. He rests his elbows on his knees and tents his fingers under his chin.

"What's changed?"

I stare at him and shake my head. "I just... The McCoys... The site."

Ethan nods his head up and down and frowns. "You look like shit."

I look up toward him and see the grin playing on his lips. "Thanks," I say. Ethan shrugs and leans back in his chair.

"You didn't answer my question. What's changed?"

I know that Ethan won't let this go. Where Dominic is too quiet, Ethan is always talking things out. He can smell a lie a mile away. I take a deep breath.

"Maddy," I say simply. "She left."

"Ahh," Ethan says. "The girl."

"She's not just a girl," I say. I feel my heart squeeze and I think of the look in her eyes this morning. She looked so hurt, and it was all my fault. "I can't explain it, Ethan. I know that she works for the hotel, but she *cares*. She cares about it all. She cares about Lang Creek. She found out about the petition and got into shit at work and she thinks I was hiding it from her."

"Were you?" I frown, staring at Ethan. He shrugs again. "Were you hiding it from her?"

"No! I mean, I signed it, but I didn't think it would come to anything. Petitions are bullshit! They never change anything!"

"Right. Except this time it did."

"For now, yeah." I sigh again and rub my temples. "I can't stand the thought of the McCoys squeezing more money from this town, but when I think of Maddy..." My voice trails off and I stare at the carpet between us. Ethan stays still, waiting for me to continue. "I care about her, Ethan. Like, really care about her."

I finally look my brother in the eye and he lifts an eyebrow. "Love?"

"No!" I blurt out. "I mean, I don't know. Fuck, man…" I sigh. Ethan chuckles.

"Look, I can't help you with her. But once this place is built, do you think she would stick around? You said yourself she's a successful engineer. What life is there for her here? She's here for one reason, and it's that fucking hotel." He pauses, and we stare at each other for a moment. I nod slowly and he continues. "When the hotel is done, when it's all over, she's going to leave, Aiden." He almost whispers the last part and I drop my head into my hands.

"I know," I say. My chest feels like it's being squeezed by a huge hand and I can hardly make my voice louder than a whisper. "I know."

"I'm sorry, Aiden. I'm sure she's nice. But look around you."

His eyebrows are drawn together and I see real concern in his eyes. What he's saying hurts, but it only hurts because it rings true. I take a deep breath and push myself up so I'm standing.

"I'm going out of town for a few days," I say, making a snap decision. "I need some time to think."

"Where will you go?"

"Don't know. Wolf Mountain, maybe. Somewhere with no cell phone towers, no hotels, and no women."

Ethan grins. He nods his chin once and reaches his hand toward me. I grab it and he pulls me in for a hug.

"Take care of yourself, Aiden," he says. His voice is muffled in my shoulder and I nod.

"Yeah," I say. We pull apart and he puts his hand on my shoulder. He looks me in the eye and for a moment I see my father's eyes in his. In a way, he's the one who's most like our dad. He's reasonable, level-headed, business-minded. He can talk to people and they like him.

He grins at me and I see my father's smile. I smile back and shake my head.

"You remember when Dad took us camping down the river and you got stuck in that tree?"

Ethan laughs. "Got stuck in the tree! More like got tricked into going up there. If I remember correctly it was you and Dominic who lifted me up there."

"You cried for the whole day and wouldn't talk to us for a week," I laugh.

"You guys were assholes," he says. "But I guess not much has changed.

I grin, and he claps me on the shoulder. "If I can survive growing up with you guys as brothers, you can survive this."

"I'll see you in a couple days," I say. He nods, and I see something in his eyes. They spark, and then there's a darkness behind them. It's gone in an instant, and we nod at each other again.

When I get into my dad's old truck, he's standing at his door waving me off. I watch him in the rear-view mirror as he turns back inside and closes his door, and it feels like the end of something.

I don't know what it's the end of, or what's going to happen, but it feels significant. I turn the truck onto the main road and head north. I'm going to drive until I find somewhere to stop, then I'm going to set up my tent and stay out there for a few days. I'm going to figure this whole thing out. Maddy, the McCoys, the hotel – I'll figure it out. I just need time to think. I need to feel the mountains and hear the birds and breathe the clean air that I grew up in. I just need a bit of time, and then I'll know what to do.

35

MADELINE

WHEN I WALK BACK into work, Barry looks up from his desk. The little patch of red skin is gone, and he nods his chin down at me. The worst of it seems to have passed. I slide into my desk and start my computer. Once it's on, I check my emails and read the report from the Department that revokes our work permit. I sigh. It's not going to be easy to reverse this one.

Barry appears next to my desk and nods his head toward the conference room.

"Can I talk to you?"

He looks almost apologetic, so I nod my head and follow him in. We both sit down and Barry takes a deep breath.

"I didn't handle that properly. I shouldn't have brought up your personal life."

I shake my head. "I should have run through the changes with you on the application. I swear I didn't know about the petition, Barry. I would have told you."

He nods. "I know. I shouldn't have accused you of that. I know you care too much about doing your job right to do something like that."

I take a deep breath and feel a tiny fraction of the weight lifting off my shoulders. Barry doesn't seem mad at me, and my dad is right. It's not my fault this project has come to a halt. It couldn't be just one person's fault.

The site is stood down, so we spend the rest of the day doing paperwork. I start working on an appeal for the petition and get to work sorting through all the conditions that have to be met for the work to be reinstated.

Before I know it, I'm right back in the swing of work, putting all my effort into getting this hotel built. It's not until I'm back in my room at the end of the day that I realize what's happened. Maybe I do want to build this thing. Maybe I *do* really believe that it'll be good for the people of Lang Creek.

I care about my job, and my job is to care about the environment while constructing these projects. It doesn't mean I'm a bad person. I stare at myself in the long mirror in my room and stand up a little bit taller. I'm definitely not a bad person. It's not evil to be building a hotel in a beautiful place. It's not going to ruin the place. It just means more people will be able to enjoy the beauty. I never would have seen this place if this hotel wasn't being built.

I never would have met Aiden if this hotel wasn't being built.

Pretty soon, my eyelids start feeling heavy. My brain starts slowing down after buzzing all day and my whole body feels more and more tired. The adrenaline and emotion of the day knocks me out, and within minutes I fall into a deep sleep.

· · ·

A LOUD BANGING on my door wakes me up. I jump up out of bed, still fully dressed in my work clothes. I fell asleep on top of the covers, collapsed in bed straight after work. I rub my eyes and head to the door, pulling it open to see Cecilia with her arm raised to bang it again.

"Cecilia, what's going on?"

"Maddy! The hotel!"

"What about it?" I look back toward my window and see the dark night sky. "What time is it?"

"It's just after midnight. I tried calling you. Barry is on his way to site with the fire department."

"What? What are you talking about? What's going on? Cecilia, slow down."

"Maddy, the hotel is on fire."

Her words almost knock me back. I take a step backward and finally see the horror in her face. A siren rushes past the front of the street in the direction of the site. I hurry to the window and pull it open, poking my head out to see a huge plume of smoke in the distance. It smells like wood burning. I glance back at Cecilia, my eyes wide and my heart thumping.

"It's on fire?"

"They're calling in the helicopters. They're saying it could turn into a forest fire. Come on, let's meet Barry."

I'm in a daze. I'm a zombie, being led down the steps and out to the car. I get in the passenger seat of Cecilia's car and watch the trees rush by as we drive toward the site. I hold my phone in my hands, and it feels heavier than usual in my lap. My finger hovers over Aiden's number, but I don't have the courage to call him. Not yet.

We're stopped before we can get to the site offices. The fire department has barricades set up, but I can see the fire raging higher up on the hill.

The heat of the fire is in the air, and the smell of smoke is strong. I look at Cecilia with my eyes wide and she shakes her head. The flames have consumed the entire hotel and are starting to lick the nearby trees. The entire site is a mess of yellow and red and orange.

From this safe distance it looks almost beautiful, in an awful kind of way. I get out of the car and watch as one of the main supporting beams at the front of the hotel collapses. We just put that in two weeks ago.

Barry's car is parked over to the side, so I walk over next to him. He's on the phone, but when he sees me, he rolls down the window and turns toward us.

"Arson," he says. My eyes widen and my heart drops to my stomach. My hand slips into my pocket and I feel my phone again.

"How do you know?"

"We won't know for sure until the fire's out and we can get some forensics, but the forest was soaked with all the rain we've gotten. The Fire Marshal said there's no way this is a natural fire. With all the opposition we've gotten..." his voice trails off and his eyes move toward the fire. He shakes his head from side to side and I think I see a tear forming.

I follow his gaze and once again I'm almost mesmerized by the fire. It's not until Aiden's voice rings in my head that the horror really starts to set in. One little thing he said last time I saw him, when his eyes were full of anger and his voice was hard and cold.

"Short of burning the fucking place down, that petition was the only thing I could do."

I can hear his voice as if he were standing next to me. It plays over and over in my head as I watch the fire destroy everything we've built.

I take a few steps away from the cars and pull out my phone. In a few quick taps, my fingers are once again hovering over his name. My heart starts pounding and the tears fall on my cheeks.

Cecilia appears beside me and wraps her arm around my shoulders.

"Come on," she says. "The smoke is getting to you. Let's get back somewhere safer."

It's generous of her, to blame the smoke for my tears. I slip my phone back in my pocket and let her guide me back to her car and pack me into the front seat. I let her drive away, and I can't bear to look at the raging fire behind us. I let her take me back to the hotel and guide me up to my room.

There, she helps me take my shoes off and pours me a glass of water. I'm catatonic. I know I am, but there's nothing I can do to change it. She finally leaves and I lie back in bed and stare at the ceiling.

I can't believe that Aiden could have done this. Was it him? Is he capable of something like this? Of arson? Of destroying something so big?

I know that he didn't want the hotel to be built, but is he a criminal?

The peaceful sleep that I had earlier seems like a lifetime ago. Now all I have is dread and horror and questions and betrayal. My mouth tastes like ash and my chest feels empty.

My phone is ringing beside me, and it takes me a few seconds to recognize the sound. I turn my head to see my mother's phone number on the screen. I move slowly, as if my limbs are suddenly twice as heavy as they were an hour ago.

"Mom," I say into the phone. My voice is hoarse and I can't manage anything else. Some part of my brain registers the sound of her sobbing.

"Your father," she says between sobs. "Your father. Come back, Maddy. He's leaving us."

I don't want to understand her, so I don't. I stare at the ceiling and listen to her crying as if it's happening to someone else.

"What do you mean, Mom? Where is he going?"

She takes a deep breath and sighs into the phone. "He's dying, Madeline. Come home."

36

AIDEN

AFTER A COUPLE NIGHTS under the stars, I'm ready to face the world again. I've heard the birds chirping and heard the crickets at night. Last night there was an owl nearby, and I fell asleep to the sounds of the wind in the trees.

I realize now that the hotel isn't the problem. The hotel might be huge, and ugly, and bring in lots of tourists that don't respect the area – but it will also bring trade and breathe life back into our dying town. The hotel could be a good thing.

The problem is the McCoys. Their opportunistic, vulture-like attitude to business has always been a cancer on this town. If I can't stop the hotel, then at least I can take back my father's businesses.

I've finally allowed myself to think about the past. Even though it hurts as much as ever, it doesn't seem as hopeless as before.

Ten years ago, Mara McCoy and I were dating. The whole town knew that we'd get married one day. My father's business was booming. He ran a small transportation business,

Clarke Transportation, with a fleet of a dozen trucks that ran routes throughout the area. The three of us brothers were set to inherit it.

Our two families were inseparable, and we'd gone down to the creek for a summer picnic. That day, Mara fell into Lang Creek and my father jumped in to save her. He was in the icy water for a little too long, spent a little too much time fishing her out. With his typical stubbornness, he refused to go to the doctor. It wasn't until the pneumonia was too far gone that he finally went to the hospital.

That's when I learned his health insurance wouldn't cover his care. He stayed in hospital until we were completely broke. The McCoys offered to buy up the business to fund his hospital care. It wasn't until he died that we realized what we'd done. They'd taken advantage of three teenage boys to acquire the most profitable trucking company for a hundred miles. They renamed it 'McCoy Trucking' and paraded the business in front of us until the three of us fled town. Dominic and I to the mountains, and Ethan away to school. The ultimate shame was having to go back and work for the people that betrayed us.

They preyed on three teenage boys. Dominic had power of attorney over Dad, but he wasn't capable of making that kind of decision. There was no lawyer, no advice, just a hastily drawn-up contract by the McCoys.

It's not about the hotel. It was never about the hotel. I'm not mad about Maddy, or her involvement in the hotel construction. When I pack up my truck and head back to town, my heart feels light again. I drive for miles, humming to myself until I get radio signal, and then listening to the radio until I get phone signal. Once my phone gets back into range, it starts buzzing and buzzing and buzzing with missed calls and text messages. I frown, glancing over at it as I drive.

I pick it up and scroll through the missed calls. Bill, my brothers, even Margaret McCoy. No call from Maddy, or anyone else from the company. My heart starts to beat a little bit harder as my phone starts to ring.

"Bill," I say, putting the phone to my ear as I drive down the deserted highway.

"Aiden, where the fuck have you been?"

"I've been up past Wolf Mountain for three days. I told Ethan I was leaving to clear my head. Why? What's going on? I've got thousands of missed calls."

"The hotel," Bills says. "Aiden, someone's burned the hotel down."

I almost drop the phone in shock. My mouth hangs open and it takes all my concentration to keep my vehicle on the road.

"Aiden? Aiden are you there?"

"Yeah, yeah, I'm here," I answer. "What... What do you mean?"

"I mean someone took a match and lit the fucking thing up like a Christmas tree. There's nothing left."

I blow out the air from my lungs and shake my head. "I'll be back in town in six hours, Bill, I'll come straight in."

"Any idea who could have done it?" he asks.

I think to the look in Ethan's eye when I left, and all the talk between him and Dominic about burning the place down. They wouldn't actually do it, would they? Ethan is a straight shooter. He wouldn't commit a crime like that. Dominic, maybe...

"No," I lie. "No idea. I've been out here for days," I say.

"Alright. I'll see you when you get in."

I hang up the phone and toss it into the cup holder beside me. I grip the steering wheel with both hands as my eyes get wider and I shake my head.

"Ethan, Dominic, what have you done?" I breathe. "What the *fuck* have you done?"

I keep repeating it to myself like a mantra. I flick the radio off and drive in silence until the road gets familiar and I finally pull into Lang Creek.

When I get to the police station, Sheriff Whittaker comes out to greet me. He extends his hand and pumps my arm up and down.

"Aiden, thanks for coming in."

"So it was arson?"

"Forensics are still investigating, but we've pretty much narrowed down the point of ignition to two sources." He looks around and lowers his voice. "If it's not arson, then I'm a fucking lady in a tutu."

I blow the air out of my nose and shake my head.

Bill chews his lip and wrings his hands together. "I hate to ask you this, Aiden, but I'm going to have to ask you to make a statement. We're asking everyone in town to make one, just to get ahead of the investigation."

My eyes widen. "You don't think that I..."

"No!" he exclaims. "No, no I don't think it was you. We just need to know your movements from Thursday morning to Friday evening." He looks around again and grins at me. "If you ask me, whoever did it is a fucking national hero."

I nod, but my face stays steady. I think back to Thursday, from the morning when Maddy confronted me to going to Ethan's house to taking off on my own. When the fire was started, I was on my own in the mountains. I don't have an alibi, and even though Bill is saying he's glad the place burned down, I know how these investigations go.

It'll be a witch hunt. Who better to blame than the poster boy who opposed the construction of the hotel? I also happen to be the guy who conveniently decided to go camping on his own when the whole thing happened? I nod to Bill and follow him into the police station. My heart sinks with every step, and I try not to think about the fact that out of all those missed calls on my phone – not a single one of them was from Maddy.

37

—————

MADELINE

I'M FINALLY ALONE. I kick off my heels and sit down on the couch in my living room. I'm in New York, and the sounds of traffic and honking and sirens are muffled from the street below.

I close my eyes and lean back, resting my hands on my stomach. My black dress feels smooth under my fingers, and I lie back and let my body sink into the couch. I spent the whole day keeping myself together as people came to me one after another to offer their condolences. For the thousandth time today, I feel like I'm on the brink of falling apart. This time, I let it happen.

My father's funeral was torture. I had to be the dutiful daughter when all I wanted to do was scream. Now that I'm alone, I don't know what to do with myself. I just sit on the couch with my head leaning against the back cushion. My eyes are closed and my whole body feels heavier than it's ever felt before. The first of my tears squeezes out of the corner of my eye and rolls down the side of my face.

I don't want to cry. I don't want to wallow and sit here alone and cry myself to sleep – only to wake up with a puffy, swollen face and a hollow chest. I don't want to be here alone. I don't want my father to be dead.

I open my eyes and let the tears fall out one after another. I don't sob. I don't move. They just pour out of my eyes one after another. I stare at the ceiling for a while, and then I lift my head and look around the room. It's exactly how I left it before I went to Lang Creek, but somehow it feels different. It feels like something has changed. Like *I've* changed.

I look at the tasteful throws and complementary cushions on the high wingback chair. I look at the little mirrored boxes beside the orchid on my coffee table. I wiggle my toes in the plush rug under my feet and it just feels so fake. My apartment is gorgeous, and impeccably decorated, but once again I'm here alone.

My father has died, work is a disaster, and the first man I've ever loved has turned out to be someone I thought he wasn't.

Why hasn't he called me?

It's been almost a week since I left Lang Creek, and I haven't heard a word from Aiden. Ever since that morning when I confronted him at his cabin, he's been completely silent. His silence has spoken louder than anything he could have said, it's just not what I want to hear.

More tears fall out of my eyes and I take a deep breath. My chest feels heavy and I force myself to breathe in completely. What does Aiden matter? What does work matter or the fire or Barry or the petition when my father just died? The backbone of our family is gone. He's the one person that I've been able to turn to, who believed in me completely even when I didn't walk the path set out for me. And now he's dead.

Over the past few days, I've learned to hate the euphemisms people use for dying. 'Leaving us', or 'passing on', 'passing away' and 'crossing over'. It's all bullshit. He's *dead*. He's not coming back. I don't want anyone to be gentle with me. I don't want anyone to coddle me and make me feel better by trying to call it something different. He died, and he's not coming back. It hurts more than anything. Calling it something other than death just feels like a slap in the face.

I've seen the looks that people are giving me. I'm expected to step into his role – to stop my own career in environmental engineering and do what I was supposed to do from the start. The company is mine if I want it, and I don't know what to do.

I don't want it. I don't want to run the company. I don't want to build a hotel in Lang Creek. All I want is my father. I want his shoulder to cry on and I want him to tell me he's proud of me and that everything will be okay.

I reach for my phone and hesitate before unlocking the screen. I take a deep breath and find Aiden's number. It takes me a long time to type out a message, and even when it's typed out, I don't hit 'send'. I throw my phone aside and finally get up off the couch.

I take a long, hot shower, and I warm up some leftovers in my fridge. I pour myself a tall glass of wine and take a sip, staring at my phone from across the room. It's right where I left it on the sofa.

I know I shouldn't send it to him. I know it'll only open up the wounds and make me feel worse. What I should do –

what everyone *wants* me to do – is to forget about Lang Creek and take care of my father's company. I should put Aiden Clarke and the McCoys behind me and move on with my life.

But as I stand here, sipping dry red wine as I lean against the counter in my fancy kitchen, all I can see is my phone. Its blank screen is taunting me, calling out to me from across the room.

The microwave dings and I glance at it in disgust. Warming up those leftovers was ambitious of me. All I want to do is take them out and throw them directly into the trash. I glance from the microwave back to my phone and put my glass of wine down a bit too forcefully.

I make a bee-line directly for my phone and grab it off the sofa where I left it. I unlock it with a swipe and find the draft of my message. My hands are trembling but I hit 'send' before I can talk myself out of it. It takes a second for the message to say *'sent'* and then another second for the word *'delivered'* to appear underneath it. I sigh and read the message over and over and over until it's burned into my mind.

My heart is thumping as I look at the text I just wrote. Part of me feels like I shouldn't have said anything, but part of me feels completely satisfied with myself. I read my words one more time before dropping my phone down and heading back to my wine. They're the exact words that I've wanted to ask him for almost a week, ever since the day I stood on the hill watching all my hard work burn to ash. They're the words that I haven't had the guts to say until now, until everything in my life has burned up with that hotel.

Did you do it?

38
———

AIDEN

BILL SAYS things like 'eliminate me from the investigation', but all I hear is 'suspect number one'. The paranoia is well and truly setting in when he leads me to a small room and asks me if I want anything to drink.

I've seen the movies. I know what happens in rooms like this. I get left here to stew for hours as they try to extract a confession from me. Even though I know that I've been camping for three days, even though I know I've had nothing to do with this fire, I still feel partially responsible.

I shouldn't have said those things to my brothers. I shouldn't have said it to Maddy! What if she told Bill that I'd threatened to burn the place down the morning of the fire? That's how people get convicted of crimes they didn't commit.

I jump as the door opens and Bill drops a steaming cup of coffee in front of me. He gives me a wink and sits down.

"This shouldn't take too long, Aiden. You'll be out of here in no time." He flicks a switch on the recording equipment. "Right, so can you state your name for the record?"

"Aiden Clarke."

Bill nods. "And where were you on Thursday night? That's the night of May 24th."

"I was out on Wolf Mountain, camping up at a site over there. I stayed there until this morning. Uh... Sunday."

"Was anyone with you?"

"No." My heart starts thumping as Bill nods, staring at the sheet in front of him.

"And can anyone confirm your whereabouts?"

"I told my brother Ethan I was going. I stopped for gas on the way there, about 1pm. I bought firewood at about 6pm from a shop at the base of the mountain."

"Up at Wolf Mountain?"

I nod. Bill points to the recording equipment and I clear my throat. "Yes."

Bill nods and winks at me. He shuffles his papers and taps them on the table. "Well, those are all my questions. Thanks for your cooperation, Aiden." He flicks the switch on the recording equipment and winks at me again. I frown, not knowing what all these winks are about. "Thanks, Aiden. All done! If you want to go see the site, I'm heading up there this afternoon."

"Sure, that sounds good," I say. Bill extends his hand across the table toward me. I shake it, and he leads me out of the police station. When I get outside, the sun is shining on my face and I look around me in a daze. I was 100% sure that I'd be in jail right now. I thought Bill would be interrogating me for hours. He didn't even look like he believed me when I told him I was camping six hours away.

I shake my head and walk toward my truck. Old Man Wilson is passing on the street and he waves to me from the other side.

"Morning," I call out. He crosses the road toward me and reaches his hand out. I shake his hand. He pulls me close with a devilish grin on his face.

"You're your father's son, you know that, Aiden? Everyone in town is talking about you."

I frown. "About me?"

Old Man Wilson grins at me and rubs the side of his nose as he winks. "That'll teach those corporate fuckers."

He shuffles off and I stare back at him, my mouth hanging open. I look around at the buildings around me and I shake my head. He thinks I did it! They all think I did it! Bill even thinks I did it! I spin around and stare at the police station. An officer walks out and looks over toward me. He gives me a meaningful nod before heading toward his cruiser.

My jaw is still hanging open. They all think I did it, and they're happy about it? No one seems upset at all. I climb into my truck and start driving down Main Street. Before I get to the end of town, I make a hard-right turn and head toward Dominic's house – a small shack right at the edge of town. I jump out of the truck and stomp toward the door.

"Dominic!" I yell as I bang on the old wooden door. "Dominic! I know you're in there!"

The door swings open and my brother's huge body appears in the opening. He looks me up and down and then nods me inside, stepping aside for me to pass. As soon as he closes the door, I spin around toward him.

"Dominic, what the fuck is going on? Did you do this?"

"Do what?" he asks innocently, walking past me to sit down on his couch. He glances at the TV before turning the volume down and looking back at me.

"Oh, I'm *sorry*," I snip. "Was I interrupting something?" I say, looking at the TV.

"Kind of, yeah," Dominic says with a grin. He pauses and then chuckles, waving to his sofa. "Come on, Aiden. Sit down."

"Tell me you didn't do this! Did you burn down that hotel?"

He looks at me and grins before shaking his head. "Don't ask questions you don't want the answer to."

My heart is thumping and I look at my brother for a moment before swinging my eyes around the room. He lives just like I do – it's simple and minimalist, but it's always clean. I sink onto his sofa and put my head in my hands.

"Everyone thinks I burned it down, Dominic. Old Man Wilson just shook my hand over it! Bill even thinks I did it!"

Dominic chuckles. "Typical. We do all the work and you get all the credit."

"Credit! It's a *crime*! We could go to jail! I didn't even do it and I'm afraid of going to jail!"

"Police don't seem to be in a hurry to catch anyone."

"What about when the McCoys start putting pressure on them? When the company puts pressure on them? They're going to want answers!"

"They'll pick up their insurance checks and run," he says with a snort. "The site will be left like that until the forest reclaims it, and no one will ever be charged."

"How can you be sure, Dominic! How do you know?"

Dominic grins and turns the volume back up on the TV. "Bill Whittaker said so himself, right before he torched the fucking thing."

"What!"

Dominic just laughs and I watch him, my heart thumping and my jaw hanging open. It feels like I haven't closed my mouth in hours, ever since I started driving back. Dominic shakes his head and laughs.

"You were always way too afraid of getting in trouble. Even as a kid. Do you remember the time you told Mrs. Wheeler that you *thought* about not doing your homework? You handed it in on time, but you still apologized for thinking about not doing it."

Dominic swings his gaze toward me and smiles as he shakes his head. "That's why we didn't ask you to help, Aiden. We had to show you the site before we did it to make you understand. I know that girl has you all twisted up inside, but that hotel would only have brought trouble."

"You guys were planning this all along? So your comments about burning it down... You were being *serious*? Bill was *in* on it?" My head is spinning. What town is this! It's like I live in the Wild West. "And wait, twisted up inside?"

Dominic just settles back into his chair. "It's for the best."

I nod and take a few moments to compose myself before standing up to leave. I run my hands through my hair and let all the air out of my lungs. I don't know what to think. If everything works out the way he says, then could they be right to have burned it down? It's such huge destruction, it can't possibly be okay…

But they did save the area from the decades of overuse and destruction that would have come had the hotel been built. They stopped the McCoys from gaining more ground in town.

The townspeople seem happy about it, at least. I mumble a goodbye to Dominic and walk out in a daze. My head is spinning. When I get to my truck, my phone buzzes in my pocket. I pull it out and look at Maddy's name. My heart starts beating faster as I read the message.

Did you do it?

As soon as I see the words, my heart sinks like a stone. I can deal with the townspeople thinking I did it. Whether they're happy, or mad, or sad about it – I can deal with them. But in Maddy's message I can hear her pain and outrage and I can't take it. I can't deal with her being mad at me.

All the feelings from Thursday morning rush back to me, and I see her face as she raced away from me. I can see her tear-streaked face. I can see the anger and sadness and outrage in her eyes. I read her message again and I feel that same emotion in those four little words.

I can only answer the truth.

No.

39

MADELINE

I WASN'T EVEN sure Aiden would answer my text, but as I stare at the word on the screen, I almost wish he hadn't. It's the first time we've spoken to each other since the morning before I left. I glance at the screen again.

No.

One word. I feel a mixture of relief and doubt. I want to believe him, but it's hard to know over text. I wish I'd waited until I could look him in the eye to ask him, but when would that be? My company is demobilizing from the construction site. We're leaving until the police investigation is completed and the insurance company sorts out the details of the claim. From the way Barry was talking, it sounds like the project might be abandoned.

Aiden and the residents of Lang Creek have won, at least for now.

There's a knock on the door and I jump. I go to the door and see my sister Bianca through the peep hole. I open the door and she lifts her mouth up to try and smile. It looks more like a grimace, but I'm sure my face looks the same right now.

"You holding up okay?" she asks. "I didn't get to talk to you very much at the funeral."

"I'm fine. Shouldn't you be with your family?" I say, thinking of her husband and child. Bianca laughs.

"You are my family, Maddy."

"Right," I say with a grin. "Come in." I pour her a glass of wine and she wraps me in a hug.

"You haven't been yourself since you took that job in the mountains," she says. I look at her and let out a dark laugh.

"Dad just died, Bianca. What do you expect?"

She gives me a look and shakes her head as she accepts the glass of wine. "You know what I mean. What happened over there? At work, in the mountains."

I sigh. I have to look away from her, but I can feel her questioning stare on my face. I drag my eyes back to her and sigh again. "My head got all fucked up. I've always thought that I was one of the good guys, but there was massive community backlash with this hotel. I started seeing one of the guys who lives in town and I just got confused. I feel like I don't know myself anymore."

Bianca's face is full of concern and she wraps me in another hug. "Come on," she says. "No one knows themselves. You're my smart, beautiful, talented little sister who was always going to have a brilliant career. And you've got a brilliant career!"

"What if I don't want that anymore? What if all I want to do is run off to the mountains and live off the land with this guy for the rest of my days? Mom already thinks I'm crazy for not taking Dad's place at the company. She'll think I've lost my mind."

Bianca laughs. "Who cares what mom thinks?" She pauses, taking a sip of wine and looking at me over the glass. "Is this guy worth it?"

I purse my lips. "I don't know. I don't even know if he wants to be with me. I left it badly. I thought he lied to me about the hotel, but I think I was just taking out my own frustration on him. He did nothing wrong. And then the next thing I said to him, after almost a week of no contact, was accusing him of burning the hotel down."

Bianca inhales and nods her head slowly. "Not the best way to leave things."

I laugh and shake my head. "No. Not the best."

"Have you spoken to him since then?"

I shake my head again. "Just sent that text a few minutes ago. He answered right away." I show her my phone and she reads the two messages. She looks back at me and shakes her head.

"Sometimes we have to just go back with our tail between our legs and apologize. Remember what Dad used to say? Only fight the battles that are worth winning."

"I've made such a mess of it all."

Bianca laughs. "You know, when I first started dating Derrick, we almost broke up about fifteen times. The only thing that kept us together was being able to apologize and move on." She smiles at me. "If he's worth it, he'll understand." She takes a sip of wine and glances at me. "Worst case, you can play the 'dead dad' card and get some sympathy."

I can't help but laugh. I know it's inappropriate. My mother would probably be outraged at a joke like that, but when everything is falling apart sometimes all there is to do is laugh. Bianca starts to giggle, and soon the two of us are bent over, sloshing our wine in our glasses and holding our sides. We laugh and laugh until my cheeks hurt and tears are streaming down my face. When I can breathe again, my sister gives me another hug and points to her purse.

"I brought some food. You hungry?"

"Starving," I answer. I put my phone to the side and help Bianca in the kitchen. I take the now cold leftovers from the microwave and Bianca laughs. We talk and laugh, and for the first time in weeks I feel like things might work out. The hotel won't be built. I can choose what I want to do with my life. I don't know whether it's staying here and working for Dad's company, or working for my own company, or giving it all up and seeing if Aiden will take me back.

For the first time in weeks, a sliver of hope shines inside me.

We eat and drink wine until Bianca has to leave to be with her family. She hugs me one more time at the door and smiles, putting her hands on my shoulders.

"You were always the smart one, but I feel like I can finally give you some advice. Go see Aiden. Talk to him, apologize, and see if he's worth fighting for."

I nod as my eyes start to water. Bianca smiles at me. "You don't have to be what everyone expects you to be. Make your own life, Mads. Just be true to yourself."

"You sound like Dad," I say as I laugh-cry in front of her. I make an awful snorting sound as I try to laugh through my tears. She smiles again.

"I know." She wraps me in a hug and I hold on to her for a few more seconds before letting her go. When I close the door behind her, I let out a big sigh and look around my apartment.

I can hear the traffic of the street, and my neighbor is banging against the wall. There's a siren wailing in the street below me. I walk over to the window and look outside at the lights and buildings and concrete and asphalt around me. I can't see any green. I can't see a single star. My heart squeezes, and Bianca's words replay in my mind.

I don't have to be what everyone expects me to be. I don't have to be the trailblazing career woman. I don't have to be the environmental engineer who saves the world. If I want to, I can be the woman who's in love with a man from Lang Creek. I can be the woman who grows her own food and worships the mountains and lives happily ever after.

That can be me, if Aiden wants me. If he takes me back. If I wasn't just a fling, and if he feels the same way about me as I do about him. That's a lot of 'ifs', and my stomach feels heavy. I'm nervous.

The thought of confronting him again scares me. The thought of apologizing and telling him that I was wrong is scary. I stay rooted in place, staring out the window as car after car after car rushes by below me. I watch the traffic lights go from green to yellow to red and back to green, and it all seems so meaningless.

He might not want me back, but I have to try. He's the only thing on this planet that seems real to me anymore. He's the only person that's ever let me explore who I am without judgement. He accepted me without any expectation that I would have a brilliant career or be anything other than myself.

I have to find out if any of that was real. I push myself away from the window and turn back toward my luxurious apartment. I have to go back to Lang Creek.

40

———

AIDEN

WHEN I WAS COMING BACK from my few days away, I felt like I had it all figured out. Maddy, the hotel, my past, the McCoys... Now, I'm sitting in my cabin staring at the walls and wondering what to do.

The thought of going back to my old life seems so depressing. Even being up here, knowing she's not a short drive away is killing me. I didn't know how lonely I was until I wasn't lonely anymore. Maddy showed me something different. She showed me that happiness is possible for me. I don't need my father's business, I don't need to hang on to my anger, I don't need to feel that pang of guilt every time a 'McCoy Trucking' vehicle passes me on the road.

I can let all that go. All I need to be happy is *her*.

When I sit on the couch, I remember making love to her on it. When I sleep in my bed, I remember how much nicer it is to have her beside me. When I stand in my kitchen, I remember that little grin on her face as she leaned against the countertop waiting for me to kiss her.

The cabin seems so small now. I drop my head in my hands and let out a breath. Would she even want to live here? She comes from the city! I saw that spark in her eye every time she walked in, but would it last? What if we're just too different?

I glance out the window and see the corner of the big house. I stand up and look at it through the window, letting the memories of my childhood flood my mind. Maybe she wouldn't be happy in this cabin, but what about that house?

I ignore the voice in my head telling me I'm being ridiculous. A bigger house can't fix things, a part of me knows that. I still pull on my boots and head up toward it. This time when I walk in, my mouth doesn't go dry. I start looking at the house with a critical eye. I inspect the ceilings and the bathrooms. I look at the kitchen and check all the fixtures. It needs some work, sure, but this house has a soul. It saw my brothers and me grow up in it. It saw my mother and father love each other and now it's been empty for a decade.

I turn on the tap in the kitchen and let the water run. It sputters and spits for a few moments, and then water starts pouring out of the tap. The old pipes sound like they're struggling under the effort, but after a couple seconds the water runs clear. I nod in satisfaction.

Suddenly, I'm like a man possessed. I walk from room to room, cataloguing all the things that need to be fixed. I grab an old piece of paper and sketch up a new layout for the kitchen and dining room. I run upstairs and rip off a piece of old wallpaper that's hanging down. I peel up a corner of carpet and smile when I see good hardwood floors underneath.

This house could be a masterpiece. It could be a home.

It would take me a while, but I could do it. I rush back to the cabin and check my phone. There's no word from Maddy. I hesitate, wondering if I should call her. I don't know what I would say, though. *Hey, Maddy. Do you want to move into my childhood home and live on the mountain with me? Do you want to leave your career behind and be with me?*

I cringe, knowing it doesn't sound like a great proposition. I know she was happy here, but happy enough to give up her life? Her career? Happy enough to get rid of all the small comforts that she grew up with?

I glance back at the big house and take a deep breath. I don't have the energy to think about that right now. I'll start working on the house, and within a couple days I'll work up the courage to call her. Maybe I can go to New York and see her in person. I never was any good on the phone.

The garage is a few steps away. I jog toward it and throw open the door. I take a deep breath. I pull on my mechanic's overalls and look down at the 'McCoy Trucking' lettering across my chest. Today, it doesn't feel like a dagger in the chest. I feel nothing. They're just words, and the McCoys are just people.

My tools are hanging neatly, calling out to me from the wall. I stomp toward them, grabbing a few and strapping on my tool belt. I head back up toward the big house. I'll start in the kitchen and work my way through it room by room.

The rest of the day is a frenzy of activity. I knock down walls, I rip out cupboards, I throw out old carpets. By the end of the day, I'm covered in sweat and sawdust and old insulation. My hair is plastered to my head and I'm breathing heavily.

The entire first floor of the house is gutted. There's a huge pile of demolition materials in the front yard. I walk over to the other stack of furniture and personal items and pull a big tarp over it for protection.

I take a final walk around the ground floor, looking at the bare timber walls and running my fingers along every stud. I spin around in a circle, smiling to myself.

It feels good to do this. It's a fresh start. It's breathing life into the house that I used to be afraid of even looking at. It's changing my future while still respecting my past. I'm letting go of the things that have held me back and looking forward.

I just hope that it's enough. I hope that I'm not wrong about Maddy, and that she felt what I felt. I'm hoping that her love for the mountains was real. I'm hoping that what I saw in her eyes was love for me. I peel my sweaty clothes off and walk into the shower.

Today, the hot water feels like it's cleansing more than my body. My mind and soul are being cleaned as well, and all that's left to do is rebuild them into something better than before. I can build myself back up as I build the old house and hope that the newer version of me is enough for Maddy.

I open my eyes and remember that day in the shower with Maddy. My cock starts to throb between my legs and I take a deep breath. I hope she wants me as badly as I want her.

Tomorrow, I'll get up and do it all over again. Every day until the house is finished, and I can show Maddy what she means to me.

41

MADELINE

MY HEART IS THUMPING when the plane lands. I have a rental car booked and I know I have a three-hour drive before I get to Lang Creek – but I'm still a nervous wreck. I can only imagine what I'll be like when I get closer.

I close my eyes and take a deep breath. My mother was outraged that I was leaving, but Bianca understood. Last night I decided to leave, and I booked the first flight out this morning. I just have a small bag with me, hardly enough for a week. I don't know how long I'll be here, or what I'll do while I am here. I shake my head and focus on what's ahead of me.

I need to apologize to Aiden, face to face. I need to tell him that he showed me a new side of myself and that he makes me a better person. I need to tell him that I love him.

My heart bounces against my ribcage as I think of saying those words out loud. My mouth is dry and my palms are sweating as I get into the rental car. If all those looks he gave me were real, and all the time we spent together was true, then he might say it back to me. He might say those three magical words and then my heart will soar.

Or, he might turn me away. I can't even bear to think about the sting of rejection right now. I need to cling onto the small sliver of hope that I'm enough and that my apology is enough. I need to listen to the voice that tells me that he wasn't lying to me about those things, that what I felt was real. I drive down the road, speeding toward Lang Creek. My head is filled with worries and hopes and thoughts and feelings. All I can do is keep driving.

By the time I get close to town, the sun is starting to set. I hesitate, wondering if I should leave it to tomorrow. I could drive up the winding road to his cabin in the morning, with the fresh light of day around us.

I shake my head at the thought of staying at the McCoy Hotel again. I can't wait until tomorrow. I have to do it today. When I see the familiar little sign on the side of the road, I turn off and start my way up. I drive back and forth with the road, trying to ignore the lump in my throat and the thumping in my chest.

The drive up to Aiden's cabin seems longer than before. It seems to take an eternity to go up the mountain, and with every bend in the road I get more and more nervous.

Suddenly this doesn't seem like such a good idea. I've never put myself out there like this before. I don't even know how he feels. We haven't spoken to each other in over a week! Yesterday I basically accused him of burning the new hotel to the ground.

I make the last turn and see the trees open up toward Aiden's cabin. My pulse is racing and my palms are so sweaty they're almost sliding off the steering wheel. I don't see any lights on in the cabin when I pull up outside. I get out of the car slowly, closing the door and taking a few hesitant steps toward his cabin.

My breath is shallow, and all the doubts start washing over me.

He isn't even here. What am I doing here? I shouldn't have come. What do I expect, that he'll change his whole life to be with me? That he'll let me move in? What would I do here?

I start breathing a bit faster and take one more step toward the cabin. My feet crunch on the gravel and my eyes start to water. I stare at the four walls where I found out what it means to be happy. My chest squeezes and it feels like I'm never going to feel that again.

With a deep breath, I walk up to the front door. I know he's not in here. There aren't any lights on and there's no smoke coming out of the chimney. But just for myself I need to knock. I need to do everything I can to prove to myself that I tried.

I lift my hand up and rap on the door a couple of times. The sound is sharp and sounds almost too loud in the stillness of the forest. My chest squeezes again and I wait for a few tense seconds before letting my shoulders slump.

He's not here.

A weird mixture of relief and disappointment washes over me. All this buildup – all the thoughts, and worries, and hopes that I thought over and over and over for the past few days have come to nothing. It's so anticlimactic it hurts. I hoped I would have my own Hollywood moment. I hoped he'd wrap his arms around me and tell me he'd love me forever.

That's not going to happen, because he's not even here. Will I have the courage to come up here tomorrow? I could just turn around and drive back toward the airport.

I sigh. He's not here. I resign myself to that fact and turn back toward my car. I keep my head down and stare at the gravel pathway, trying to hold back the tears in my eyes. I feel almost foolish for coming all the way up here. The gravel crunches underfoot and I'm lost in my own thoughts when the sound of his voice makes me jump.

"Maddy?"

He sounds almost hesitant. My head whips around and I see him standing there, at the edge of the clearing. He's wearing his work clothes and has a bead of sweat rolling down his face. He looks like he's been working hard, with his hair plastered to his forehead and his shoulders covered in dust. He wipes his hands on the front of his coveralls and takes a step toward me.

"What are you doing here?" he asks. I open my mouth and suddenly my words are gone. I don't know how to answer his question. I don't know how to put my feelings into words and I don't know what to tell him. I can't tell if he's happy or sad or mad to see me.

I open and close my mouth like a goldfish as he closes the distance between us. His face is dark and unreadable and as he gets closer my heart starts to thump harder and harder. With every step, my voice seems to get further and further away.

God, he looks good.

He's just a couple feet away from me, and all I want to do is run into his arms. He stops walking when he's a step away from me. His eyes search mine and we stand there, inches apart, saying nothing. I open my mouth and my voice comes out as a hoarse whisper. I can only manage two words as I stare at the man I love, the man who makes me want to change my life.

"I'm sorry," I whisper.

Something snaps between us and in an instant his arms are around me and he's crushing his lips against mine. He pulls me into him as I wrap my arms around his neck. I inhale his scent, loving the musk that fills my nostrils. A shiver runs through me as his fingers sink into my flesh. HIs tongue plays with mine and he kisses me harder than ever before.

I can hardly breathe. All I can do is keep my lips on his. My fingers tangle into his hair and he growls as I pull it gently. He drops his hands to my ass and pulls me closer so that I feel his hard cock pressed against me.

Finally, we pull apart and stare at each other's eyes. We're both panting. His chest is heaving up and down with mine as his arms squeeze me closer. I run my fingers through his hair and he groans in satisfaction.

"You came back," he growls.

My eyes are prickling and all I can do is nod. "Yeah," I reply, still not able to talk above a whisper. Without another word, he dips his chin down and takes my lips in his. I close my eyes and melt into him. My heart is flying and my head is finally calm. I'm home.

42

AIDEN

I KNOW I SHOULD SHOWER, or I should take my dirty work clothes off. I'm filthy from another day of working on the house. Right now, all I can do is kiss her and touch her and convince myself that she's real.

Holding her in my arms is the sweetest pleasure. Feeling her body tremble and seeing her eyes shine makes me want to howl into the night. I pull her closer and crush my lips against hers. Her body fits perfectly into mine and for the first time since she left, I feel whole again.

I drop my hands to her ass and hoist her up. She giggles and wraps her legs around my waist as I turn toward the cabin. I kick the door open, breaking the doorknob as splinters of wood spray into the cabin.

"I'll fix it tomorrow," I growl, not taking my eyes off her. She laughs and runs her fingers through my hair, squeezing them into fists and sending pleasure and pain through my skull. The sensation sends a thrill all the way down to my cock and all I want to do is plunge it into her. I carry her to the bed and lay her down, lying on top of her and covering her in a million kisses.

I missed her moans when she was gone. I missed the way her body trembles when I touch her, and the way her eyes blaze with desire. I missed the way she breathes my name when I touch her. I run my hand between her legs and I can feel the heat of her center through her pants. She moans gently and pushes her hips up toward me.

I don't know why she came back, or how long she'll be here, or what she wanted to tell me – but right now none of that matters. All that matters is her body next to mine.

I stand up and tear my coveralls off. They drop to my feet and I watch as Maddy pulls her jeans off and lifts her shirt over her head. The air in the cabin is cold, and my eyes drift to her hard nipples. My cock throbs and I lean down to take one in my mouth. She moans as my lips touch her breast, wrapping her fingers in my hair and reaching her other hand down to stroke my cock.

I'm so hard it hurts. My whole body is pulsing for her. She looks at me with fire in her eyes and then everything is a blur. She's screaming my name and arching her back. She's pressing her body into mine and wrapping her arms and legs around me. Her nails are digging into my skin and every touch is making my body more electric. I kiss, and bite, and lick anything I come in contact with.

We're animals. I push myself into her with the full force of my desire for her. Her body melts into mine and mine into hers. I'm inside her, around her, beside her. We're one. We make love until everything is spent, until she comes and I come and our bodies are more connected than they ever have been. We make love without saying a word to each other, letting our moans and bodies guide us.

Her body is more perfect than I remember. She feels softer than I remember, and she tastes sweeter than she did before. It's not until we're lying side by side and the breath comes back to our bodies that we look at each other. She smiles and trails her fingers over my chest. I groan, catching her fingers and pressing them to my lips.

"You came back," I say, searching her face for answers. She nods. I watch her swallow, peering into my eyes and breathing softly. Her lips part slightly and her eyes get brighter.

"I love you," she says. I hardly hear the words, she says them so softly. To my ears though, they sound as loud as a scream. My mouth curls into a smile and I wrap my arms around her, pressing my lips against hers and feeling my chest rumble.

"I love you too, Maddy," I finally say when we pull apart. Her eyes water and she smiles at me, running her fingers through my hair and trailing them down my cheek.

"I'm sorry," she says. "For everything. For doubting you. For accusing you of lying to me. For asking if you burned the hotel down. It was me who was wrong. I was taking my own confusion out on you and it was wrong."

I shake my head. "Maddy," I say, pressing her fingers to my lips again. "You don't need to apologize. I'm just happy you're here."

"What happened?" she says slowly. "At the hotel?"

I take a deep breath and shake my head. "It sounds like it was a bit of a group decision in town," I say slowly, not wanting to name any names. Not yet, anyway. "I took off after you came here. I went camping up north to clear my head and when I came back it had burned down."

She nods, running her fingers through my hair. "Are you happy it's gone?"

I stare at her, wondering what she wants me to say. I can't read her face, so I decide to just tell the truth. "Yeah," I say. "I'm glad it burned down."

Maddy looks at me for a moment and then I see a grin creeping across her face. "Me too," she says softly. I laugh, and my body relaxes a bit more. Her lips part again and she takes a deep breath. "Can I stay?" she asks, again barely above a whisper. I can't help it, I start laughing. I wrap my arms around her and laugh until she's laughing with me, and then jump out of bed. I pull on some pants and a sweatshirt.

"Come on," I say. "I want to show you something."

She frowns, but doesn't ask any questions. She pulls her clothes back on and I interlace my fingers into hers. I lead her out the cabin and up the path toward the big house. She glances at me and I look down at her, smiling. I nod to the house, opening the front door and letting her step through.

I've made good progress. The whole bottom floor is bare and ready for construction. I walk in after her as she looks around.

"Over here is going to be the living room, open concept with the kitchen. I'm going to put the kitchen counters over here, with an island in the middle. We can have a small bathroom over here, and dining table here. I was thinking we could build a patio and have a place to have breakfast in the morning."

Maddy opens her mouth to speak but all she can do is shake her head in amazement. I grab her hand again and lead her upstairs.

"There's four bedrooms. Here's the master. I'll take the carpet up and get a good rug. The wallpaper can go, obviously."

"Aiden..." Maddy breathes. She turns toward me, her eyes shining bright as she wraps her arms around my neck. "Are you serious?"

I laugh. "I just gutted my childhood home. Yes, I'm fucking serious," I growl, touching my nose to hers. Her smile widens and she laughs with me.

"This is incredible! Can I help?"

"So, does that mean you're staying?"

Maddy grins and nods her head slowly. "I was thinking I could start a garden shop. I liked working at the community garden. I've got a bit of money," she says, glancing around. "Actually, I've got a lot of money. I was thinking we could have a garage and a garden shop in town. Maybe a small hardware store." She glances at me and my heart starts to beat a little bit faster.

"A garage?" I ask slowly.

She nods. "If you want. We'd be business partners, obviously. Fifty-fifty. But I was thinking there's nothing in town like that. There's enough traffic and surrounding communities that would need a mechanic like you who has his own garage."

I laugh and pick her, spinning her around in our future bedroom. I kiss her one more time and wrap my arms around her. We sway gently from side to side, smiling at each other. There are so many things that are unsaid between us. We'll have to have so many conversations, get to know each other so much better. Somehow the thought of it excites me. I know that I have all the time in the world to tell her about my past and to learn about hers. I kiss her once more, and decide to ask her one of the thousand questions I have for her.

"Why did you leave so quickly?" I ask her. "Was it because of me? The rest of your coworkers stayed way longer. Some of them are still here."

Her face falls and she shakes her head. "My dad died," she says. Her voice is tense and she looks up at me. "I had to go home for the final days and the funeral. He was sick, remember? I told you. He took a turn for the worse. I got the call the night the hotel burned down."

"Maddy..." I breathe. My heart squeezes for her and I hold her tight. She shakes her head.

"It's okay. I wish you could have met him. He'd have loved you. I think he just wanted me to find my own way, or my own place in the world."

"And that place is Lang Creek?" I ask, my voice tight as I hold the woman of my dreams in my arms.

She laughs and shrugs. "It's wherever you are," she finally answers. This time when I kiss her, it's more tender than before. It's a kiss that knows I'll be able to kiss her again tomorrow, and the next day, and the next. It's a kiss that says I'm truly and completely hers.

EPILOGUE
MADELINE

ONE YEAR LATER...

The whole town shows up to the grand opening of the new shop. I look at the big sign at the front: C & C Home and Hardware store. Clarke and Croft. People are already calling it C&C's, and it feels like we've been accepted into the community. It probably helps that everyone thinks Aiden burned the hotel down. Everyone except the McCoys were celebrating for weeks.

He finally told me that his brothers and the sheriff were the ones who did it. I didn't know how to react. I still don't know what to think of it. It's wrong, obviously. Arson is never right. But somehow it feels appropriate here. The hotel was like a stain on the mountainside, and now it's gone. The company decided to take the insurance money and abandon the site. There's been a half-assed remediation attempt, but for the most part it's been left to the forest to reclaim. The police investigation never solved the crime, obviously. Sheriff Bill Whittaker has had a bounce in his step for a whole year.

I glance around at our new shop and shake my head. I'm a small business owner in a small town. It's nowhere near as prestigious as working for my father's company, or being a rising star as an environmental engineer, but I don't care. I've realized that none of that matters. Aiden has taught me what *does* matter, and that's love, and life, and wilderness.

There are balloons, and music, and food, and drink. Everyone comes in to see the new store. Aiden is beaming, wearing his new branded "C&C's" shirt. I've never seen him as happy as when he got rid of the old coveralls that had the McCoy name on the front.

Old Man Wilson comes up to me and shakes my hand. "You did a great job with the place," he says to me, glancing around. "And a great job with the man," he adds with a wink. I laugh, looking over at Aiden again. He's smiling and talking more than I've seen him do since the day I met him.

My heart feels light. Aiden appears beside me and slides his arm around my back. He kisses my temple and I melt into him. I'll never get tired of being in his arms. The front door jingles and in walk Mara and Margaret McCoy. Aiden tenses beside me and I rub his back to help him relax. They look around the shop and saunter over to us.

"Congratulations," Mara says with the same fake smile as her mother.

"Thank you," I respond. The four of us stand there awkwardly.

"So I guess you're our new competition," Margaret says as she looks Aiden up and down.

"I guess so," Aiden responds. "Back to the way it was before."

Margaret purses her lips and I squeeze my arm around Aiden. I can feel the tension in his body and I know how hard it is for him to keep his cool. He's stiff until Mara and Margaret nod, turn around and walk out. Aiden and I exchange a glance. He sighs.

"I'm going to take back Dad's business," a voice growls behind us. I turn to see Dominic staring after Margaret and Mara. He glances at Aiden. "I know that you've moved on, and I'm happy for you. You should enjoy your new life. I'm not ready to move on, though. Not yet."

"What are you going to do?" Aiden asks. He stares at Dominic for a few moments and I feel like there are wordless things being said between them. Dominic cracks first as a grin breaks across his face.

"I'm not going to burn the McCoy hotel down, if that's what you're asking."

Aiden laughs and shakes his head. "Just don't get yourself into trouble."

Dominic nods and glances at me. "I'm happy for you. For both of you." He wraps his arms around me in a big bear hug. I laugh and try to pull away when the breath feels like it's being squeezed out of me. He finally lets me go and winks at me. "Take care of my brother."

"Will do. Take care of yourself."

"Always." He shakes Aiden's hand and heads off out of the shop. I glance at Aiden and he shakes his head.

"I can't control him," he says with a shrug. "I just hope he doesn't get himself into trouble."

I don't know what to say, so I rub Aiden's back in response. We turn back to the customers and greet and smile and laugh until CC's grand opening is over.

My eyes are closing after an exhausting day. I can hardly stay awake as we drive up the mountain, back up toward the cabin that I now call home. I know every twist and turn and by the time the car stops I'm ready to collapse into bed. Aiden glances over at me and smiles.

"Come on," he says. "I want to show you something."

I know that look in his eye, and I can't say no. I take a deep breath and force my eyes open as I get out of his truck, following him up the path. When the big house comes into view, my jaw drops. For the past three weeks, Aiden hasn't let me anywhere near it. I had no idea he was done. He lets me in the front door and the ground floor steals the breath out of my lungs.

It's tastefully decorated, with old and new furniture. The whole place is open, and I can see the gleaming new kitchen at the back of the house. My hands fly up to my face as I look around. I finally look at Aiden and shake my head.

"Aiden, it's…" My voice trails off and I take a step into our new home. "It's beautiful."

"You like it?"

"Like it?" I say. "You did this?"

Aiden laughs. "I had some help."

"I feel like I'm on *HGTV* or something," I say with a laugh. "This is incredible!" I'm like a kid, running from room to room and squealing over everything. I helped him choose the finishes and paint colors and furniture, but seeing it all put together is better than I could have imagined. There are a few picture frames on the shelf in the living room, and I see a photo of my dad next to one of his. My chest tightens and Aiden puts his arm around my shoulder. He kisses my forehead and the two of us look at the pictures of our fathers, side by side in the place of honor on the shelf. He takes my hand and guides me up the steps. He opens the door to the master bedroom and the tears finally start falling down my cheeks.

I have a new home, a new business, and a man that I love. I didn't know happiness like this was possible. Aiden wipes the tears off my face and wraps his arms around me.

"What do you say we christen the new bed," he says with a wink. I laugh and tilt my chin up toward him. When he kisses me, I feel happier than I've ever felt before. I'm more than happy. I'm in love, and I'm finally home.

～

Grab your own exclusive bonus chapter:
https://www.lilianmonroe.com/subscribe

SWEAR TO ME

THE CLARKE BROTHERS SERIES: BOOK 2

1
———

DOMINIC

I LOVE the smell of sulfur that hits my nose when the match bursts to life.

I watch the tiny flame for a second as it shifts and dances in the light breeze. I glance up at the sky, littered with a million stars, and then down to the huge, looming building in front of me.

I can smell the gasoline soaking into the ground and into the timber at my feet. The luxury hotel is like a stain on the side of the mountain. It shouldn't be here. Still, as I stand here with the match in my hand, I can't help but hesitate.

My brother Ethan drops his match. I hear the whoosh and crack of a new fire coming to life across the construction site. Sheriff Whittaker is next, igniting the north side of the building. I watch the two fires start to lick at the new construction. They climb up the bare beams and travel along the trails of gasoline that we sprayed all over the ground floor.

The match is burning close to my fingers. I watch the small flame for a second more, and finally drop it at my feet. I take a step back as the gasoline ignites. It starts as a low blue flame, traveling fast along the fuel that I just splashed over the ground. A deep sense of satisfaction wells up inside me as I watch the fire ignite. I'm transfixed, watching the flames as they dance along the side of the half-built hotel. The heat of the fire starts to warm my face and clothes until it's almost too much. When it starts climbing up the beams, I turn away and walk back toward the trailhead where we came from.

Ethan and Bill are already there. They nod at me, and the three of us turn toward the building once again. We watch it in silence until the flames have overtaken the half-constructed luxury hotel.

"Let's get out of here," Ethan says in a low voice. I grunt in response and turn back toward the trail. We walk in silence, waiting a few minutes before fishing our head lamps out of our pockets and turning them on. It's a two-mile hike before we get to the old logging road where we parked our trucks.

When we get there, Bill extends a hand toward me. "Good work, Dominic. Ethan. I never thought I'd commit a felony as Sheriff, but I can't feel guilty about this one. That hotel would have been the end of this town – and the end of these forests as we know them."

"It's better off gone," Ethan replies. Bill nods his hand and heads toward his truck. I jump into mine and Ethan gets into the passenger seat. The engine rumbles to life and the two of us head back down toward the town of Lang Creek.

We crest a hill and I see the fire burning behind us in my rear-view mirror. I stop the truck and jump out. Ethan follows. We climb into the bed of the pickup and watch the fire burn for a few minutes. As the flames lick higher and higher, the corners of my lips start to lift up with it. A siren wails in the distance, and Ethan and I exchange a knowing look.

Gradually, a laugh starts rolling through my chest until my shoulders are shaking and I'm throwing my head back. I clap my brother on the back and he grins at me.

"I can't believe we fucking did that," I finally say as I shake my head.

Ethan laughs. "I can."

"Let's go," I finally say, staring at the fire one last time and shaking my head. As we drive away, the smell of smoke lingers in my nostrils and I grin. It's a crime, and it should be wrong, but it feels so, so right.

ONE YEAR LATER...

I LOOK at the dregs of beer left in the bottom of my bottle and I sigh. It's probably time to go home now. My brother Aiden and his new wife Madeline are cuddling at the long table with stars in their eyes.

It was a great ceremony and a beautiful wedding that the whole town came to. I'm happy for him, of course. He's my brother. How could I *not* be happy for him? He's found a beautiful wife, started his own garage and hardware store in town, and finally found happiness. After ten years of grief following Dad's death, that's something to celebrate. I just can't shake the feeling that something isn't right.

Maybe this sour feeling in the pit of my stomach is just plain old jealousy.

I jump when Bill Whittaker puts his hand on my shoulder. He hands me a new beer and I nod in thanks.

"Why the long face, Dominic? Aren't you happy for your brother?"

"Delighted," I say. "Just tired, I think. Long day."

Bill takes a seat next to me. He spreads his legs wide and sighs. It's strange seeing him in regular clothes. He's usually wearing his dark blue uniform and wide-brim hat. Even when we snuck through the forest to burn down that damned hotel, he was in uniform. He looks over at Aiden and Maddy and nods.

"They make a good couple. Aiden deserves a bit of peace."

I don't bother looking over at my brother and his new wife. I grunt in response and put my empty beer bottle down on the table in front of me. The plastic chair groans underneath me as I move, and I wonder how long until it collapses. It probably wasn't made for someone my size.

Bill stares at me for a few moments. "Are you okay, Dominic? Ever since that whole thing with the hotel..."

"I'm fine," I interrupt. "Fine."

Bill stares at me and nods his head a few times. "Are you having regrets?"

"Regrets?" I say, shifting my weight again and looking at him. I snort, and for the first time in hours, my lips curl into a grin. "Not a fucking chance."

Bill laughs and raises his beer toward me. I clink my fresh bottle against his and smile again, shaking my head. "Best thing we ever did was burn that thing down," I say before taking a sip.

"Yup," Bill replies.

The two of us fall into a comfortable silence and I think about that night last year. The whole town was up in arms about the new luxury hotel being built on the outskirts of town. When it burned down, it was like everyone celebrated for weeks. Everyone except the McCoys, obviously. They owned part of the new hotel before it *unfortunately* went up in flames.

People suspected my brothers and me, and the three of us were treated like heroes. Aiden didn't have anything to do with it, but it's not the type of thing you talk about after it's done. I hadn't expected that much attention. They still look at me differently, even a year later. It's almost like a sort of reverence.

The McCoys haven't said a word to me since the whole thing happened, and I'm not complaining. They keep to their side of town, and I keep to mine. I still have that deep, endless desire to get even with them, but I don't know how.

I shake my head to pull myself out of my reverie and nod to Bill.

"I'll see you around, Bill. Time for me to head home."

"Take it easy, big fella."

I stand up and stretch my body. I've been working hard at my workshop lately, and every muscle in my body is screaming for rest.

"Hey," Bill calls out as I turn away. I look over my shoulder at him. "You heard Mara McCoy's coming back?"

I frown as I think of the McCoy girl. I shake my head. "No, is she?"

"Due back any day now. Didn't work out with her rich businessman."

I grunt in response before turning away. Why is he telling me that? Why would I care? Something stirs in the depth of my stomach as I think of the McCoy girl, but I shake my head and ignore it.

It takes a few minutes to say my goodbyes, and I breathe a sigh of relief when I finally head down the mountain toward my little cabin on the outskirts of town.

As much as I love my brother, and as much as I'm happy for him, I can't wait to be back in the peace and quiet of my own four walls.

2

MARA

"The car is waiting outside, ma'am," Claire says. I look at my fiancé's personal assistant and nod. Well, *ex*-fiancé's personal assistant, I guess.

I zip up my last suitcase and stand it up. Claire makes a move toward me, but I hold up a hand.

"It's okay, I'll bring it down."

"Sure," she says. She's a true professional. This whole time, she's kept a straight face and helped me as much as she could as I moved out of this beautiful house. I've called this place home for the past two years, and now I'm being thrown out like some kind of squatter. Vincent didn't even have the decency to come here himself. He sent his assistant to deal with me, and that stings almost as much as the breakup.

I swallow my bitterness and square my shoulders. Lifting my chin up, I wheel the last of my suitcases out the door. I hear it click shut behind me and Claire's footsteps follow a few seconds later. We walk down the hallway in silence, both staring straight ahead. Not a word is spoken between us until we walk out the front door and get to the car. The driver grabs my suitcase from me and packs it into the trunk before opening the back door for me.

I have one foot already in the car when Claire clears her throat. I look at her, wondering what other ridiculous request Vincent has made. I almost feel sorry for her. *She* still has to put up with him.

"Miss McCoy," she says, hesitating. "For what it's worth, I thought you were wonderful. I'm sorry –"

"Don't apologize, Claire," I say as a pang passes through my heart. "It's not you that should be sorry. And for the last time, call me Mara!"

There's a hint of a grin on Claire's face, and she nods her chin down once. "Mara, then. Good luck."

I climb into the car as the driver shuts the door. He slides into the driver's seat and thankfully doesn't say a word to me as we head toward the airport. We drive through the winding roads, packed with mansion after mansion before we get onto the freeway. I watch the buildings go by and bid a silent goodbye to Silicon Valley.

Maybe this is for the best. I'm not a California girl. Never was, and probably never will be. I've never fit in here. I'm from a tiny town in the heart of the Adirondack mountains, where the trees are old and the mountains are older. I take a deep breath and close my eyes, leaning my head back on the headrest.

A tear falls from the corner of my eye and I quickly brush it away. I didn't think it would end this way, and the shock of it still hurts almost more than the fact that it's over. Like a fool, I thought Vincent actually loved me. I thought he'd wanted to spend the rest of his life with me. Like a fool, I thought the construction of the hotel at Lang Creek was secondary to our relationship. I thought that luxury hotel brought us together, and *love* united us – not the money the hotel would bring.

I was wrong.

It stings – the rejection. It makes my heart squeeze and my cheeks burn when I think about it. How could I be so stupid? I should have known at the very beginning. I saw Vincent's demeanor change from cold and distant to charming the instant the hotel deal was on the table. I should have known it wasn't love.

I was nothing but a pawn that my parents used. *Again.*

Another tear escapes my eyes and I brush it away angrily. I set my jaw. I'm not going to let that happen again. I won't be used and sold off to some rich businessman just so my parents can profit off it.

That hotel burning down was the best thing that ever happened to me. Now I know who Vincent is, and I won't be married to him for the rest of my life. Now I know that my parents think they can use me for their own personal gain.

The bitterness seeps into my veins and I savor the taste of it. I've been such a fool. I've believed I was loved and appreciated for who I was, but I've only ever been loved for what I have. And now? What do I have? A broken engagement, no money, no prospects... I've got nothing. I have to go back to the people that put me in this position in the first place.

My parents got a tidy sum from the insurance company when the hotel burned down. That helped ease their fury at the whole thing. They still haven't forgiven the Clarke brothers, but what can they do when the Sheriff himself won't do anything about it?

I smile as I think of the small-town politics I'm about to fly back into. It's like a hornet's nest, and for the first time in my life I'm going back with my eyes wide open. I know who my parents are. I know how they've built their business and made their money, and I know that it hasn't been from honest, hard work.

I don't want to be a part of that – but for now, I need some time to get back on my feet. I'm still reeling from Vincent breaking off the engagement, and my head spins whenever I think of my parents.

I just need some time to figure everything out. I need to figure out who *I* am and what *I* want. I won't be used in any other business deals. I won't be sold off to the highest bidder and then returned when it all falls to pieces. I'm going to go back home and tell them *exactly* what I think of them.

The driver pulls up to the airport departures and hops out of the driver's seat. By the time I've climbed out of the car, he's found a cart and started loading my bags onto it. He smiles at me sadly and touches his cap.

"Good luck, Miss McCoy."

"Thanks, Will. Take care."

I grab the handle on the cart and set off toward the airport's sliding glass doors without looking back. My heart is beating and my mouth feels dry as I check into my flight and make my way through security. I never thought I'd be this nervous to go home.

When the plane lifts off the runway, I watch the brown and green hills fall away beneath me. I catch a glimpse of the ocean before we turn east and I bid it another silent goodbye. My heart feels a little bit lighter when I think of the mountains I'm heading back to. My lips curl into a smile and I rest my head back in my seat. I close my eyes and take a deep breath. All I breathe is stale airplane air, but I can almost taste the sweet, fresh air of the Adirondack mountains. In a few short hours, I'll be home.

~

Get Swear to Me here:
https://www.lilianmonroe.com/clarke-brothers-series

Sign up for my reader list for a bonus epilogue from Lie to Me:
https://www.lilianmonroe.com/subscribe

ALSO BY LILIAN MONROE

For all books, visit:

www.lilianmonroe.com

Brother's Best Friend Romance

Shouldn't Want You

Can't Have You

Don't Need You

Won't Miss You

Military Romance

His Vow

His Oath

His Word

The Complete Protector Series

Enemies to Lovers Romance

Hate at First Sight

Loathe at First Sight

Despise at First Sight

The Complete Love/Hate Series

Secret Baby/Accidental Pregnancy Romance:

Knocked Up by the CEO

Knocked Up by the Single Dad

Knocked Up...Again!

Knocked Up by the Billionaire's Son

The Complete Unexpected Series

Yours for Christmas

Bad Prince

Heartless Prince

Cruel Prince

Broken Prince

Wicked Prince

Wrong Prince

Lone Prince

Fake Engagement/ Fake Marriage Romance:

Engaged to Mr. Right

Engaged to Mr. Wrong

Engaged to Mr. Perfect

Mr Right: The Complete Fake Engagement Series

Mountain Man Romance:

Lie to Me

Swear to Me

Run to Me

The Complete Clarke Brothers Series

Garrett

Maddox

Carter

The Complete Rock Hard Series

Doctor O

Doctor D

Doctor L

The Complete Doctor's Orders Series

The Cause

Second Chance: A Rockstar Romance in North Korea

www.ingramcontent.com/pod-product-compliance
Lightning Source LLC
Chambersburg PA
CBHW010552170726
48285CB00011B/2866